T0029736

OFFER OF REVENGE

AN AMERICAN MERCENARY THRILLER

JASON KASPER

SEVERN RIVER PUBLISHING

Copyright © 2017 by Regiment Publishing.

All rights reserved.

No part of this book may be reproduced in any form or by any electronic or mechanical means, including information storage and retrieval systems, without written permission from the author, except for the use of brief quotations in a book review.

Severn River Publishing
SevernRiverBooks.com

This is a work of fiction. Names, characters, businesses, places, events and incidents are either the products of the author's imagination or used in a fictitious manner. Any resemblance to actual persons, living or dead, or actual events is purely coincidental.

ISBN: 978-1-64875-485-2 (Paperback)

ALSO BY JASON KASPER

American Mercenary Series
Greatest Enemy
Offer of Revenge
Dark Redemption
Vengeance Calling
The Suicide Cartel
Terminal Objective

Shadow Strike Series
The Enemies of My Country
Last Target Standing
Covert Kill
Narco Assassins
Beast Three Six

Spider Heist Thrillers
The Spider Heist
The Sky Thieves
The Manhattan Job
The Fifth Bandit

Standalone Thriller
Her Dark Silence

To find out more about Jason Kasper and his books, visit
severnriverbooks.com/authors/jason-kasper

To James Sexton

Who survived the Quiet Hell with his head unbowed,
and emerged an even better man than before.

Welcome back, brother.

OFFER OF REVENGE

EXILE

Omnia iam fient fieri quae posse negabam

-Everything which I said could not happen will happen now

1

September 9, 2008
María Montez International Airport,
Dominican Republic

Wood grain patterns collided and diverged into a greater labyrinth, an orderly chaos forming a tapestry upon which I could project any number of illusions. Embracing this welcome distraction from the monstrous heat, from the never-ending wait, from the rattling tension pulling on a brain too far removed from its last drink, I saw tidal waves crash and turn to sand dunes, clouds merge into a storm, Karma's face appear and then vanish behind a veil of rain.

Her face had been an inescapable shadow trailing every thought since my arrival to the Dominican Republic one month ago.

Or had it been two?

I didn't know anymore. The sun's progress across the sky before it yielded to damp, windswept periods of darkness had long since blurred into a kaleidoscope of depression and alcohol, of writing and contemplating the abyss my life had become since Karma's death. The loss of Boss, Matz, and Ophie was equally painful, but nothing could have stopped them from embarking on their final mission. I was forever sentenced to an eternal shame for living while they didn't, but free from the crowning sin of failing to save them.

I had no such reprieve from Karma.

I returned to my seat beside her in the truck often, without warning, my vision filled with the horrifying moment of her end just as vividly as if I were still seeing it in person. Only when I drank myself into a blackout shroud of numbness—a fleeting state that became increasingly harder to attain—did those ceaseless replays subside into an aching, muted dread.

I pinched the sweat-soaked bridge of my nose with my thumb and fore-finger, then placed my entire hand over my eyes and squeezed against my pulsing temples until the pressure on my skull became unbearable.

If I had asked Karma to take our combined earnings and leave with me before that mission, she would still be alive. If I had told Ian to move our getaway truck fifty feet down the trail, she would still be alive. If I had conducted a security patrol while waiting for the ambush team instead of sitting in the truck with my rifle barrel resting on the floor—

"*Lo cuarto don, 'al favor.*"

The voice beside me sounded impatient, as if this were a repeated request.

It may well have been, given that my gunfight-torn hearing was infinitely worse in the presence of background noise.

The hectic airport lobby wasn't helping—the vacuous space, from the tile floors waxed between the arrival of passenger jets to the low ceiling glaring with whatever fluorescent lights remained functional, echoed every footstep, rumble of luggage wheels, burst of laughter, and episodic chatter of the women behind the ticket counter.

Releasing the pressure on my temples, I felt the dull throb of my headache returning. September in the Dominican was the wrong time and place for a daylight return to sobriety. Unmitigated by a dive into the open water or escape to an air-conditioned room, the feverish heat turned the semi-open lobby into a sweatbox for the mind and body.

I lowered my hand from my face and returned my gaze to the wood grain surface of the table in front of me. "*Veta a la mierda.*"

At this, I heard a flat *clack* and caught a glint of metal being waved in my peripheral vision.

I looked over to see a dark-skinned hand loosely holding a switchblade knife. Following the slender arm upward with my eyes, I saw the face of an adolescent boy looking at me expectantly. He may have been any one of the two dozen boys playing stickball in the trash-strewn fields I had driven by on my way to the airport.

He flicked his chin upward. "*Lo cuarto mamaguevo, ahora.*"

Glancing behind him, I saw four younger boys standing at a distance, their arms crossed as they evaluated their ringleader's performance.

I continued studying the wood grain of the table and repeated, "*Veta a la mierda.*"

Then I felt his palm slap me upside the head—too light to be painful, too brisk to be playful—as he muttered, "*Quédate con tu mierda, mamaguevo.*"

He vanished from my periphery, his fading footsteps blending into the sound of the crowd before both were drowned in the whooshing howl of an approaching passenger jet.

I slid my legs out from the table and stood before approaching him swiftly from behind. His friends tried to warn him, their urgent faces preceding words lost amid the fever pitch of the jet touching down and roaring toward the terminal. My would-be mugger had just started to turn and look my way when I grasped a fistful of his coarse hair and swung him sideways.

He careened off his feet, his head striking the corner of a table as a spray of blood erupted onto the tile floor.

As he fell, I pulled the immense .454 revolver from beneath my shirt and stabbed it toward the teens now running to help their friend. Their advance halted as suddenly as if they'd hit an invisible wall, the flurry of flailing arms and cringing expressions going stock-still as I twitched the front sight from one boy to the next. Five pairs of eyes were fixed on my pistol, its proportions surely exceeding any handgun they'd ever heard of, much less seen, as I pointed it at their chests from ten meters away.

I turned to the fallen boy, who now appeared even smaller as he curled into a fetal position, both palms covering the side of his head as the plane outside quieted for taxi.

Dropping to my knees beside him, I swatted away one of his hands and pressed the tip of the barrel into his left eye socket.

"Where do you want it, *amigo*? The eye?" I cocked the hammer, releasing the cold symphony of the cylinder locking into place, and aligned a jacketed hollow point with his brain. "No, not your eye. You saw me just fine, but you didn't notice the fucking elephant gun under my shirt."

Lowering the barrel to his pursed lips, I applied pressure to his teeth. "What about the mouth?"

His eyes were wild, the left one marred with the redness of a hundred tiny vessels strained by the barrel's intrusion.

"No, you didn't have any problem running your mouth." Then I leaned down to his face, so close I could smell his garlic-tinged sweat, and whispered in a quaking voice, "That's it...I know where the problem is."

Scraping the barrel around the side of his bloody head, I pushed the muzzle into his ear and used the gun to tilt his head sideways against the ground. I weighted the barrel downward until I heard a sound like crumpling wrapping paper as his ear folded flat against his skull.

"You have a problem listening. I told you to fuck off. Twice. Now I'm going to show you what—"

"*POLICIA!*"

I took a long breath. My heart hammered as the blinding grip of rage loosened, if only for a moment, to reveal that a cavernous silence had descended upon the lobby. No sound from the passenger jet remained. Looking up, I saw a police officer aiming an automatic pistol at me with trembling hands.

Everything else seemed frozen in time. The ticket women were nowhere to be seen, and the remaining travelers were staring at me with expressions ranging from shock to outright horror.

"*POLICIA!* DROP THE WEAPON!"

Exhaling, I looked at the boy on the ground and muttered, "Start paying attention to who you're trying to rob, *amigo*, because there's not a cop in this country who'll be able to save you from me a second time."

I lifted my shirttail with my free hand and holstered the revolver.

Then I reached into my pocket, inciting the officer to tense his grip on the pistol with renewed determination as he shouted a flurry of Spanish words. He fell silent as I withdrew a thick roll of pastel bills as multicolored as Monopoly money that was compressed into a tight cylinder by a single rubber band.

I tossed it at him and stood, my knees popping.

"Thief," I said, pointing to the kid on the ground.

The officer knelt and hastily pocketed the cash, then holstered his gun and began handcuffing the youth. I glanced around. The group of teenagers had long since abandoned their friend to his fate.

After hoisting the kid to his feet, the officer proceeded to make a stage production out of restoring security to the lobby, heralding loud proclamations in Spanish as he marched his prisoner toward a door behind the counter. I knew the kid would be released long before his sunset game of stickball. Had he managed to rob me, he would have given the officer a cut for turning a blind eye to the mugging. There was a reason the safe house where I lived, located within a guarded community of fugitives and misfits, existed in this part of the Dominican Republic. In this tropical ecosystem of petty crime and false appearances, no one was innocent.

Least of all me.

I wearily reclaimed my seat as tourists and locals began crossing the lobby once more, heading toward the counter as the airport staff quickly returned to business as usual.

An old woman with a wooden cross suspended from her thick neck and a battered suitcase in her hand slowed as she passed me. Her weather-beaten face seemed frozen in a matriarchal sneer of disapproval, though she managed to narrow her eyes even further to shoot me a contemptuous glare.

I asked her, "What does '*mamaguevo*' mean?"

She said nothing.

"*Mamaguevo*," I repeated, snapping my fingers for emphasis. "If you're going to stare at me with that stupid condescending expression, at least help me understand your shitty culture."

She made a loud clucking noise, a well-practiced maneuver that served as her final judgment, before she turned her back on me and swayed off toward the counter.

It was at that moment I saw Ian.

He walked amid a crowd entering from the terminal, casually rolling his luggage behind him while his eyes swept the lobby. Although he spotted me almost immediately, he continued taking in his surroundings with an alert nervousness.

Diverting from the line of travelers heading toward the exit, he approached me.

His wiry frame moved beneath a bright red T-shirt and sunglasses hung from his collar—everything from his shorts to his sandals suggested an ignorant gringo tourist.

He stopped beside me.

I didn't get up. "What does 'mamaguevo' mean?"

He squinted, tilting his lean face as he examined my eyes. "It means cocksucker."

"Huh. You sure?"

"David, you look pretty rough. Do you want to get some coffee?"

"I already sobered up for this, Ian. So it better be good. Come on, let's go to the house."

Ian resolutely shook his head. "Not the house."

I shot him a glare. "Contrary to what the in-flight magazine told you, there aren't many places in this part of the Dominican without mobs of street urchins looking to mug tourists. So if you don't want to go to the house, then where exactly do you suggest?"

* * *

The beach was little more than a crescent sliver of barren sand, its narrow expanse isolated between steep, jagged hills behind us and the infinite blue sea beyond. The murky shoreline vanished and reappeared under the pulsating ebb and flow of groaning surf as I turned to survey the terrain rising behind us, feeling a tingle of anxiety creeping up my spine until it burst across my shoulders.

The palm tree-blanketed heights looming over us had become a two-dimensional shadow silhouetted by the sunset casting its final rays over the sand. Ian and I were illuminated for anyone to see, and yet he continued walking toward the waterline, oblivious, before taking a seat. I crossed the beach and stopped beside him, sliding my hands into my pockets as the early evening heat dissipated with the sun's fall from the sky.

Turning to survey the shadowy ground behind us once more, I said, "So instead of going back to the house on a secure compound, you've brought us to a piece of completely open ground where a dozen snipers could be watching us right now. If you're trying to get me to have a fucking panic attack, you're doing an astounding job."

Ian observed the dim sky over the Caribbean Sea as if seeing something remarkable, but I saw only a hazy mist of white with a sheet of darker clouds drifting beneath it moving slowly toward the shore.

He closed his eyes for a beat, his face still turned toward the sky. "No one's watching us, David. And I can't trust the house. Now please, sit down."

"I don't want to sit down, Ian. I'm ready to get revenge, so let's hear this great plan of yours."

He didn't respond, instead removing a small, round tin from his pocket and palming the lid as he pinched some of the brown powder between his thumb and forefinger. He inserted it into his right nostril and sniffed, then repeated the process with his left before seamlessly capping the tin and sliding it back into his shorts. I watched a vein near his balding temple shift as his jaw settled. "I need you to sit down now, because you're not going to like what you're about to hear."

I lowered myself onto the sand beside him, gathering my knees under my elbows. "Ian, the team is dead. Karma died next to me. The Handler is still alive despite the efforts of whatever clowns you sent in to kill him. So I'm going to go out on a limb here and say things couldn't be much worse."

"There was a survivor."

The air in my lungs suspended mid-stream. My mind turned those four words over.

"You mean one of the Five Heads."

Ian wouldn't meet my eyes and instead stared hollowly at the sky beyond the waves. "No. A member of Boss's team survived."

"That's not possible."

"I made contact with a source who used to work for the Handler's organization. He's in exile, and he shares our motivations. And he told me there was a survivor from Boss's team."

I flexed my shoulders back, feeling my spine pop. "Why do you believe him?"

"Because I never mentioned Boss's name. He has no idea I ever worked with Boss or that the name meant anything to me. It wasn't an attempt at manipulation. He was stating a fact."

A row of pelicans flying single file coasted just above the water, one breaking free from the formation and diving into a white crest of surf. I inhaled a lungful of warm, salty air and said, "We both heard the Midnight call from Boss's own voice over the radio. Matz and Ophie were in the car with him, so all three were killed. No doubt about it."

"The longer I stay in this business, David, the more I distrust everything I thought I knew about people. There was a betrayal, and that means we heard what someone wanted us to hear."

Raising a hand to silence him, I shot back, "You didn't know those guys like I did, Ian. None of them would have betrayed the others. Surviving and escaping the attack, maybe, but—"

"Whoever survived is now working for the Handler."

Long ranks of white foam charged to the shore, dispersing into nothingness as the succeeding waves followed them to oblivion. My stomach began a freefall of dread.

What did I miss?

I canvassed my memory for some sign of betrayal over the course of our months together, searching a fast-forwarding litany of personal moments— Matz shoulder-checking me as we transferred equipment from our truck to Joe's plane, Ophie breathing slowly after decapitating Luka in the basement, Boss calling me an arrogant little cocksucker in the kitchen of our safe house.

I had been brutally kidnapped by those men, surviving only because I could help them kill, and yet I'd gone on to accept their sales pitch in full. Karma told me as much when we shared cigarettes on the porch behind the team house.

I see the way you look at them...you're buying it hook, line, and sinker.

I had unknowingly lived in the midst of a traitor.

I cleared my throat. "Who does this guy say it is?"

"He doesn't know a name."

"I want to meet your source."

"Good. Because he's the only one who can get you a job interview."

"For what?"

"I told you there was one path to the Handler, and I wasn't sure either of us wanted to take it. I was referring to infiltration."

A contemptuous laugh escaped my lips. "Infiltration? If you can't even get me close enough to kill him, they're not going to let me join his inner circle."

"Of course not. If these people work how I think they do, the only insiders are family—you're an outsider, and you'll always be an outsider. But his organization has a wide reach, and they have a process for hiring low-level guys as expendable assets. That process begins when the organization contacts you, and my source has the ability to make that happen."

"And then what? I'm supposed to waltz in there with a fake name and hope they don't realize who I am?"

"All we have to fabricate is a cover story for the summer you spent with Boss's team. And that's easily explained—you spent some time hiking the Smoky Mountains after your discharge from the military, did some soul-searching. You spent a lot of time there in high school, so you know the area. We can substantiate it with photographs, and it justifies your bank accounts going untouched for a few months."

The face of the water shuddered as a gale of wind approached. I thought of the dark confines of the house I would return to that night, a space beset by the revolver I now wore on my side. Its barrel had met my mouth on several occasions to date, my life reduced to a cylinder-spin of chance no less dangerous than what Ian was proposing.

"David." Ian looked uneasy, his eyes darting across my face as he waited for a response.

"What?"

"What do you think?"

I looked skyward. "I don't know who wants me to die more—you or me. Because this is going to get me killed as surely as if I shoot myself in the head."

"I've done the legwork, and believe me when I say that infiltrating the organization—however we can, and however long it takes—is the only play we've got."

"You have a single contact who is probably lying to you. That's not a play—it's a prayer. The first thing they're going to figure out is my shitty cover story, which will get me tied to a chair and tortured to death like that poor fuck Ophie killed in the basement. Even if the story works, and I become—what were your words?—an *expendable asset,* then I'm still no closer to the Handler than I am right now. And even if your source isn't full of shit, what happens if I run into this so-called survivor—"

Ian cut me off, raising his voice for the first time since I'd known him.

"I *told* you over the phone I wasn't sure either of us wanted this path, and you flipped the *fuck* out on me. Then I work miracles to find the one person who can get you an interview and fly down here to tell you about it, only to find you so shit-faced that I don't know whether to tell you about the survivor or take you to the hospital for alcohol poisoning. So guess what—you don't like it? Then take me back to the airport and don't fucking do it."

I looked at him, my jaw falling before I said, "I'm going to kill them both. The traitor and the Handler."

"The paths to both are the same. I'm telling you, we have no options left."

"A few days ago you seemed pretty goddamn confident that the team you sent in after the Handler would succeed. What happened to them?"

"David, when this is over, I'll show you the footage. Until then, the less you know the better."

"If they all died, how do you have footage?"

"You'll understand when you see it."

I shook my head. "Give me a goddamn break. Just show me, Ian. Enough tap dancing."

"First, you need to meet with my source and convince him you're worthy of his help. Then, if we're lucky, he gets you an interview within the organization."

"And then what?"

Ian gave a somber shrug. "That's something we won't know until you make it there. I should say *if* you make it there, because, judging by your current state, I'm not terribly confident that you will. But if you manage to get a view from the inside, you're going to have to tell me what it looks like."

My thoughts jumped from the house, to the revolver, to the faces of the team before darkening with the notion of a living traitor to Karma, someone whose guilt for her death exceeded even my own.

Whatever the truth, Ian was my only link to it and to the reality that existed beyond the compound where I had spent the last miserable expanse of my life, writing and drinking as my will to survive eroded as steadily as the shoreline.

My mind leapt to a jarring, unsolicited vision of Karma's head exploding, and I felt my entire body jolt.

"You okay?" Ian asked.

I took a breath. "I'll get hired, Ian. Don't worry about that."

"I hope you're right, David. I hope you're right." He fell silent, and I said nothing to fill the void.

Suddenly I felt exhausted, consumed by an immense weariness that encompassed both mind and body. The evening air grew heavier and cooler, and while the storm clouds hadn't yet formed I knew they were coming. Before long, another rainstorm would congeal out of nothingness, masking the sun's final descent before vanishing as quickly as it had come and leaving a gleaming night sky in its wake.

2

September 26, 2008
Redwood National Park, California

My neck crawled with the certainty I was being watched, a sensation made all the more unsettling absent the comforting weight of gun metal on my side.

The peculiar feeling had spiked minutes after I had set off on the trail and since then had remained an undercurrent that hummed within my bones. As I walked, my vision shot between tree trunks of prehistoric dimensions that stretched upward to impossible heights. They rose from a sea of bright green ferns clouded by hazy whispers of fog, the collective depths of the forest forming an ever-shifting portrait of possible hiding spots and surveillance points.

Ultimately, my every attempt at detecting outside observation was futile.

I continued examining my surroundings nonetheless, the narrow trail threading between expanses of gnarled tree bark covered in verdant moss. Each breath filled my lungs with thick, humid air while the sound of flowing water grew louder ahead of me. As I proceeded toward my destination, my thoughts reverted to the certainty that had been plaguing me in the weeks since Ian's shore-side revelation of a survivor: I was going to kill Matz.

That realization had followed the torment I felt while agonizing over which of the friends I'd been mourning without end had actually betrayed the others. While all were unlikely candidates, I'd come to the conclusion that Matz, by far, deserved the most suspicion.

He had been utterly appalled by my refusal to abort Saamir's assassination, which, to him, had been just as unforgivable as leaving the female eyewitness alive. Matz had cited both decisions as justification to banish me from the team, and he harbored no illusions about what that would have meant—hell, he referred to me only as "Suicide," dismissing my pleas for continued employment.

We're not a depression rehab center.

Although he and I had raced into a target house together amid grenade blasts and engaged in close combat with twice our number of armed bodyguards, he had maintained an open disdain for me until the last night I saw him. After our final dinner together before I parachuted into the mortar point in our grandiose plan to kill the Five Heads, Matz had openly told me he didn't care if I lived or died. His only concern was that I initiated the attack on time.

But would he have been able to kill Ophie? Boss? Karma, his own sister?

I glimpsed a small footbridge ahead, the sight of which fractured my thoughts and returned my mind to the task at hand.

The bridge's rickety wooden frame was suspended above a turbulent channel of water that coasted atop a bed of smooth stones. I approached the bridge without crossing onto it, then turned left and departed the trail.

Stepping high amid dew-covered ferns that soaked my pants from the knee down, I followed the stream deeper into the forest. The burbling ripple of water beside me did little to mask my movement as shadows overtook the ghostlike glow of sunlight illuminating the fog between the trees. With each step, I was burdened with an increasing feeling that I was approaching certain death, which threatened to slow my progress every bit as much as the vegetation I was wading through, unarmed and unaccompanied as per the source's instructions. The dense forest and total isolation left me unable to defend myself or, indeed, even run from danger.

Yet I continued off the path, approaching a meeting with the fountain-head of information that had compelled me to return to America.

My mind's eye turned to Ophie.

He was far harder to envision as the betrayer.

Ophie had stood up for me at every turn during my first weeks with the team, when there was absolutely nothing for him to gain. In the wake of my killing of Saamir against orders, Ophie was the sole voice in favor of continuing to train me. And, after the final team meal together, when he and I were the last two left at the dinner table, he had expressed a profound concern for Matz's well-being. So steadfastly had he resisted suspicion that I could only think of one reason for his possible betrayal.

Ophie was supremely intelligent, and, for all his projected nonchalance, he unquestionably possessed both the intellect and the flippancy capable of toying with the newest team member—me—for his personal amusement. He had expressed a certainty that he would live, albeit within a discourse on the meaninglessness of the natural order as he had experienced it in combat and elsewhere. Then there was Karma's ultimate assessment of his motivations, which had no basis in loyalty or honor.

To him, this is slightly more fun than deer-hunting.

Diverting around a tree, I stopped at a face-height streak of bright yellow on the bark. Examining it more closely, I saw the shape belonged to a foot-long slug with narrow, trembling tentacles inching gradually down the redwood and toward the ground.

A man called out, "State your endgame."

My heart leapt. The voice was ubiquitous, the damp forest concealing any echo as the words hung in the space between the trees, heavy as moisture in the air.

I replied, "I seek a seat at the table."

"Which table?" The words were lilting, singsong—a Pakistani or Indian accent, I thought.

"His."

"To what end?"

"The final one."

"That road is long."

I rolled my eyes, deciding that the speaker must be Indian. "I'm ready to travel it."

The figure of a wide man stepped out from behind a tree perhaps fifteen feet away. Though I couldn't make out much of him—his body clad in a navy coat, his mouth cloaked in a scarf, his head concealed by a ball cap pulled low—my first, inexplicable feeling was one of revulsion.

Beneath the shaded bill of the hat, deep-set eyes examined mine closely, flicking from right to left. "We shall see."

I squared my shoulders at him. "You told Ian there was a survivor from my team."

"And I am telling you one thing more: by the end of this, you will come face-to-face with him."

"You didn't tell that part to Ian."

"And neither must you. He will not let you proceed."

"But you will?"

His reply was immediate. "I have no choice. You are not the first I have sent. None have emerged."

"If there is a survivor, he would kill me on sight. How am I supposed to get past that?"

"I do not know. I only know that you must."

"Who is he?"

"I do not know. But he was not killed with the rest of Boss's team, and he ensured the death of the others. And he now serves the one whose table you seek."

"Why should I believe any of this?"

"Because you will see it unfold as I say it will."

"If you're lying to me, I'm not going to forget it."

"Revenge is fear disguised," he said, rolling the *r* sound as if for dramatic effect. "Any clever man would disregard it when this truth occurred to him. But if you seek it, you must be prepared to do all. To die unto yourself, to be born again into acceptance of those you hate most, and even to love."

I heaved a long sigh. "All right, man, I like arcane riddles as much as the next guy, but let's cut the shit. What can you tell me that will actually help me get into this fucking organization?"

The Indian was silent for a moment, his eyes never moving from mine. "No one applies; they are sought and contacted. I will have someone reach out, and you must follow their instructions exactly. At the test, it is up to you."

"How can you get me an invitation if you're in exile?"

"That is not your concern."

"You have a fellow conspirator on the inside. Someone who hasn't been detected yet." The man's posture straightened, his coat taut against his round stomach. "Well, he better be good," I added. "So, let's say I get hired. Who will I be working for?"

"You know who."

"I want a name."

His accent spilled forth in an urgent sequence of shifting pitches. "He is many things to many people. To his workers, he is the Handler. To his inner circle, he is the One. To his enemies, he is *Khasham Khada*. And that is the name you must never repeat unless you are facing certain death, for to use it otherwise will just as likely kill you as—"

"*Khasham Khada*?" I said.

He froze.

I smiled. "If this guy is so ruthless, then how are you still alive?"

"You tell me, David. How does one escape an enemy such as this?"

A branch snapped behind me, and I whirled around but saw nothing.

Turning back to the Indian, I said, "I have no idea."

"By the end of your journey, you will. Now go."

Then he turned and moved away from me, following the stream as it crawled deeper into the forest.

* * *

As I walked from the trailhead into the parking area, the car door opened and Ian emerged.

He set his arms on the roof of the car. "You don't look thrilled."

"Good guess." I let myself into the passenger side and slammed the door.

Ian did the same, then glanced at the mirrors before turning to me. "Tell me everything he said."

I rubbed my hands together. "Well, let's see. He had an indecipherable Indian accent, he talked in circles, and he couldn't actually answer any of my questions. I felt like I was on the line with a call center in New Delhi."

Ian said, "The accent was Punjabi. That means something very different. Now quit fucking around and tell me exactly what he told you."

"All right, we exchanged his stupid bona fides, which were worthless anyway because no one else would be walking straight to that random point in a national forest. Then he said I wouldn't be the first person he'd sent to kill the Handler, and that none had come back, before he launched into a mythical diatribe about being prepared to do anything for revenge."

"What else?"

"He said I would be contacted by the organization for some kind of test. I asked how he could get me an invitation if he was in exile, and he wouldn't answer. So I said he must have a conspirator on the inside—"

"What did I tell you about mentioning that?"

I shrugged unapologetically. "It was my meeting, Ian."

"And what did he say in return?"

"Nothing, but he got quiet really quick after I said it. I know it's true. Then he said the Handler was also known to his inner circle as the One, and to his enemies as *Khasham Khada*. Does that mean anything to you?"

Ian cocked his head slightly, his brow furrowed as he considered the question. "No."

"Me neither, but he got pretty upset when I repeated it. And I asked him how he was still alive if the Handler was as dangerous as everyone seems to think, and he just said that by the end of my journey, I would know. Then he left. Frankly, I think he missed his calling as a fortune teller."

"What else did he tell you?"

My mind flashed to the Indian's proclamation that I would come face-to-face with the survivor, which was followed in short order by him forbidding me to tell Ian. I looked at Ian's anxious eyes amplified by thin glasses, the veins standing in sharp relief on either side of his forehead, and briefly considered whether he would really stop me from moving forward with the mission if I revealed that particular prophecy.

Almost by way of a response, I heard Boss speaking of Ian, just as he had when we sat in the kitchen of our final safe house.

Everything's scary to him. That's why you have us.

Boss: the last candidate for the title of betrayer.

The simple fact was that Boss knew he was going to die, and he told me so in no uncertain terms the night before the team's last dinner. Though his prophecy came from a simple dream about a ship, I saw firsthand the degree to which he believed in his end. After he and I had unexpectedly met over drinks after twenty-four hours of being awake, he told me, *One of us is going to die on the next mission, and this time I think it's going to be me.* He had even warned me that I would be assuming his position, or something like it, should the business be around long enough. The next day, after he excused himself early from dinner, I went to his room to find him crying as he stared at a picture of his smiling twin daughters.

After all my rumination, Boss remained the one team member I could not accept as being behind the team's betrayal.

I blinked distractedly, my vision once again filled with the redwood trees rising beyond the windshield. "That was it, Ian. He may as well have told me nothing at all. But as long as I get the call to join the organization, he's done his part."

I looked over to see Ian's face visibly reddening.

"Hey, fucker," he shot back, "you have less than a ten percent chance of success. That means a ninety percent chance that you rat on me and my source, and then we'll be hunted down and killed. The only reason the Handler's organization doesn't know about me already is that Boss's team handled all the direct communication, and look how that turned out. I wouldn't expect you to understand if you hadn't seen it happen. But you watched Boss and Ophie and Matz laugh in my face when I tried to warn them about the Handler—"

"You think that hasn't occurred to me a hundred times a day?"

"—and now you're doing the same thing. So don't underestimate the gravity of what we're trying to do here. Because my worst fear is that you're going to share the same fate despite my best attempts to protect you."

I shook my head slightly. "You think this is harder than it is because normal people like you have your attachments, your egos, and your concerns about family or home or a warm bed. Stop caring whether you live or die, and when, and everything else becomes simple. So is this."

In truth, my thoughts were becoming clouded, murky with an infinite number of possibilities of betrayal, of double- or triple-crossing by any one of the people I had met since my attempted suicide less than four months ago. They were dizzying in their number, impossible to contemplate individually before a competing thought invaded. Then, as soon as I had considered that new idea, it would be ousted by a successor eager for my attention.

Ian looked sullen, withdrawn, his hands now tucked into his jacket.

I regretted having to keep information from him. He had supported the team at every step along the way and was now putting his life on the line for revenge when he could have simply abandoned me instead. In a way, his act of reaching out to me in the Dominican Republic had saved my life as surely as being part of the team had.

And for those reasons alone, Ian had been a member of the team all along.

I slapped him on the shoulder. "Come on, Ian, I'm starving. Let's go get tacos."

3

October 23, 2008
Newark, New Jersey

I watched my breath slip away in long white clouds as I strode down the sidewalk toward the neon sign spelling *KONTIO'S TAVERN*.

My coat felt insufficient against the still night air, its temperature quickly sinking toward the freezing point. I glanced about the empty street, looking for my contact person but seeing no one. Distant traffic noise from the interstate was soon buried beneath the thumping bass notes as I approached the bar and a single car passed me without slowing. Slightly less discomforting than the extreme cold, I thought, was the smell. The mingled scents of chemical plants, car and plane traffic, and landfills clotted into a single pervasive odor that hovered somewhere between burning rubber and rotten eggs.

I reached the recessed door of the bar, stopping outside it as instructed.

As soon as I did so, the lone figure of a man appeared from an alley down the street. He walked toward me with a casual gait, his heels clicking on the sidewalk at a methodical tempo. As I saw his tall, lean form move closer, I felt a pang of fear.

Both the gait and body type belonged to Ophie.

I stood in disbelief, first and foremost that I would encounter the survivor on my very first meeting with the Handler's organization, and, more critically, that the betrayer was Ophie rather than Matz.

I pulled my bare hands from my pockets and kept them visible in the frigid night as I faced him with a neutral stance.

He must have wanted to talk. My identity was no secret. I had received the recruitment call on my personal cell phone after reinstating the number upon my return from sabbatical in the Dominican. The caller had addressed me by name before providing rendezvous instructions to this tavern in Newark. If Ophie had wanted me dead, there was ample opportunity to make it happen without confronting me face-to-face.

But as the man drew closer, his countenance materialized under the streetlamps and I saw that he wasn't Ophie after all. Neatly combed hair and a goatee framed handsome Hispanic features, and as he stopped next to me I estimated he was in his mid-forties.

He said, "How you doing?"

"Never better. You?"

"You here because you got the call?" His voice was gravelly, with the slightest trace of Latino intonation.

"Yes. I'm David Rivers."

"Sergio."

We briefly shook hands. "Pleasure to meet you, Sergio."

"So, why did you agree to this?"

I shrugged, stuffing my numb hands back into my coat pockets. "I cut my teeth in the Rangers and then got a medical discharge. And I can't handle a desk job after going to war."

"What are you looking for?"

"Combat. However I can get it."

"Is that what you think we do?"

"If it's not, then we're wasting each other's time."

"Fair enough, David. I'm going to lay out some ground rules right now, out here. Then we can go in and warm up, have a beer, and get to know each other. Okay?"

I nodded. "Sure."

"We're not interested in training you. We want to see your existing capabilities. If you mention my name or speak of me in any way, you're out. If you get arrested or detained in any way, you're out. If you do well, you'll receive another phone call at some point in the future. Until then, your task is to do one thing and one thing only: whatever you're asked. Let's get inside."

We passed through the heavy door into a dim, narrow room with warm air that was a welcome change from the bitter cold. The smell was likewise a reprieve as I inhaled equal parts stale beer, burned ribs, and fried seafood. A long bar divided the display of beer taps and liquor bottles from the patrons filling the room to half-capacity, their murmured conversation drowned amid '80s rock. A few people looked up briefly as Sergio stopped me just inside the door with his hand on my arm.

I looked at him, seeing in the murky light that his black hair and goatee were speckled with gray. "See that man in the black coat?" he said.

I followed his gaze to a table in front of the bar, where a massive bald man wearing a black leather jacket over a hoodie sat facing our direction. His ears had the warped appearance that came from years of being mashed into a wrestling mat, and the flat bridge of his nose indicated at least a few past breaks. His mouth spread into a wide smile, baring long teeth, as he broke into laughter at the words of an average-sized black man seated across from him whose dreadlocks were pulled into a dense ponytail.

I said, "Who is he?"

"He's the biggest guy in the room, and right now that's good enough. Your first test is to knock him unconscious and escape."

With these words, I felt a surge of unexpected relief. The looming dread of uncertainty had evaporated with the simple task at hand, and, far more significantly, I was not facing the showdown with Ophie I had been certain of a minute ago. Instead, I would channel the turbulent rage and sheer force of will motivating my search for the traitor, much less the Handler, into a simple bar fight.

I stifled a grin. "No problem. This will be fun."

Sergio gave a curt nod. "You have three minutes to make contact. Time starts now."

He started his watch and looked at me expectantly.

Turning, I calmly negotiated the narrow space between the bar and the tables while casting a sidelong glance at my target and his friend. Finding the single open stool beside the bald man's table, I hurriedly took a seat.

"'Scuse me," an older brunette in a denim jacket said from the neighboring barstool, "I'm saving that seat for my girlfriend."

I plucked a twenty from my wallet and set my elbow on the bar, holding the folded bill between two fingers as I suavely glanced at her. "Sweetheart, I'll show you two magic tricks and be gone before your friend even gets here. And if I'm wrong about that, drinks for you and her are on me for the rest of the night."

She hesitated. I could see her mind churning as she tentatively spun a finger around the lip of her glass.

I leaned in. "Skeptical? Sure you are. What I am going to perform for you tonight is an illusion called the Open Bottle. And for my second trick, I'm going to disappear."

By then, the bartender had made his way over and snatched the twenty from my hand. He leaned over the bar and called, "What can I get you?" over a wailing guitar solo screeching from the house speakers.

"What's your name, sir?"

"I'm Terry."

"Terry, have we met before?"

"No."

"I would like you to select a bottle of beer from the bar. Any bottle of beer, at random, and leave the cap on it."

He procured a bottle from the fridge behind him, then set it on the bar and slid it toward me.

"Terry has selected a Harpoon IPA. Ma'am, would you agree that this is a standard bottle, normal in every way?"

The brunette nodded, slowly blinking mascara-coated eyelashes. "Sure."

I picked up a thin bar napkin, then unfolded it and delicately draped it over the bottle. "When I remove the napkin, the bottle will magically be open."

Taking a deep breath, I placed both elbows on the bar and held trembling fingertips a few inches from the beer with an expression of intense concentration. Then I relaxed, gave a sigh of relief, and smiled. Grasping a corner of the napkin between two fingers, I announced, "I give you...the Open Bottle!"

I whipped off the bar napkin with a flourish, letting it flutter to the ground behind me.

Unimpressed, the woman glanced from me to the beer and back again.

"The bottle cap's still on, dumbass."

I looked at the cap as if it had appeared out of nowhere. "You're absolutely right. Well, maybe this will work."

Grabbing the neck of the bottle, I rotated it upside down and stood from my stool. Without warning, I whirled around and smashed it into the bald man's head as hard as I possibly could.

The bottle didn't break.

From across the table, his friend looked at me with an unmistakable expression of pity as all conversation in the bar ceased in one climactic moment. I swung the bottle into my target's head once more with the same effect—the sparkplug of a shaved skull reverberated with the strike, but the bottle remained intact in my stinging hand.

The bald man set both palms flat on the table, pushed back his chair, and stood as I cocked back the bottle a third time. He turned to look at me —he was only about a head taller than I was but outweighed me by close to one hundred pounds—just as I swung the bottle above his ear.

He caught my forearm in the viselike grip of his left hand, his cold gray eyes locked on mine. I threw an offhanded jab into his throat and then swung my knee toward his groin. Before it connected, he launched a lightning-fast right hook into my cheekbone.

My vision melted into ringing blotches of color.

The blow should have sent me flying across the room but failed to do so because—and only because—he still held my right wrist in his hand. I spun downward in a wide arc, dangling from his outstretched arm. The next few moments were a blur, but I was vaguely aware of his hands on my coat followed by the peculiar sensation of flying as my view canted sideways and he receded into the distance.

I hit the bar, bounced once, and crashed into the far wall.

A few liquor bottles rained down from above, slamming into me as I shielded my head. I scrambled to grab a fifth of Wild Turkey from the floor, then leapt to my feet and whipped it toward my adversary's head in a sharp overhand throw.

He leaned sideways and easily dodged the bottle, though it struck the chest of an onlooker, who went tumbling to the ground.

I ducked to grab another bottle and had just risen again when I was tackled from the side first by one large man and then another.

They pinned me to the ground, and I heard one of them shout over the bar, "Viggs, you want to press charges?"

With my face smashed into the filthy tile below me, I heard my target's voice for the first time.

"On that kid? He didn't even hurt my feelings. Take him out the back door, let him sleep it off in the alley. And I'll need a new round at my table."

With that, I was hoisted up and dragged into a dingy kitchen, past the smell of smoking ribs and frying seafood. I fought wildly to escape the bouncers' clutches, Sergio's words hanging heavy over my world in the frenzied moments of desperation that followed.

If you get arrested or detained in any way, you're out.

* * *

I was dragged kicking and flailing down a back hall toward a gunmetal-gray door that swung open to reveal a narrow staircase leading down.

"Watch your step, asshole," one of the bouncers said, throwing me down the stairs face first.

I barely had time to tuck my head into my elbows. My body rolled in a tumbling fall, brutally impacting against the hard corners of the steps with increasing tempo until I crashed into a concrete floor.

I curled into a half-fetal position as the bouncers descended the stairs, their footsteps barely audible over the sound of a strained groaning noise that I gradually realized was coming from me. Strong hands on my shoulders, my feet dragging against the concrete, I strained to take in my surroundings through a cloud of pain. Lights overhead sent spikes to the back of my ringing skull as my jacket was stripped off and my pockets were emptied. Then I felt the cold clasp of a handcuff tighten around my left wrist.

They hoisted me up and pushed both arms over my head before closing the other handcuff tightly on my opposite wrist, suspending me upright. The boundaries of my vision were blurred as I shifted my narrow focus upward and saw that the chain of the handcuffs was wrapped over a ceiling pipe. One of the men bound my ankles together with duct tape, and I squinted through the darkness to see cases of beer stacked along the far wall. Then a knife appeared before my eyes, the blade turning downward as my shirt was cut from my torso.

A voice in a thick Jersey accent called, "Whoda fuck is this?"

The speaker entered from a doorway to my right, pausing for a moment before he cautiously approached me. He was deeply tanned and easily in his forties, with creases around his eyes and close-cropped silver hair. He examined me with a look of mild interest.

One of the bouncers said, "He jumped Viggs upstairs."

"Jumped Viggs?" He released a chuckle of disbelief, then snatched my wallet from the bouncer and pulled out the driver's license. "David Rivahs, Virginia. Jesus. Run the address and find out 'bout his family. Call the other joints, see if they've had any action. If this is the start of something, I wanna respond fast."

"You got it."

"And you know the other thing?"

"Yeah, I'll tell him." The bouncer took my license and then vanished through the doorway with his partner.

I gazed weakly behind me, half-expecting to see Sergio in the corner, watching. But the room was empty. I had to be within the realm of the test, right? An evolving scenario with a wide cast of players evaluating my performance, perhaps.

If it wasn't, I thought, then I had just failed in spectacular fashion.

I looked back at the man, who reached into his slacks to withdraw a lighter and a pack of Marlboros. Plucking a single cigarette, he lit it and inhaled deeply before blowing the smoke toward the ceiling.

"You know," he said lazily, "couple years back they banned smoking in bars. By April you couldn't even smoke in a casino, but that got repealed last month. Which is great for Atlantic City, but here in Newark? I gotta come down here. All the way down to the cellar to burn one without freezing to death this time of year. You believe that?"

"You seem pretty confident I won't report you."

He took another drag and blew the smoke sideways. "After the ban, I ended up doing a lot of work down here instead of in the back room upstairs. At first I hated it—it's dark, dusty, no ventilation. But I came to love it here. You can probably guess why."

"Why don't you explain it to me, Cancer?"

"Well I'll be down here balancing my books, okay? You know, running the numbers, whudevah. And just when I think my night couldn't get more boring, you know what I hear?"

"A body falling down the fucking stairs."

Cancer whipped the cigarette out of his mouth, his expression lighting up as he regarded me. "Exactly. A body falling down the fucking stairs. Just the *thump-thump-thump*, getting louder all the time, and then that final crash. Then you guys always groan at the bottom. Can't help it, I suppose. Now I ain't gonna lie to you. All that sudden banging around scared the shit outta me the first few times, okay? But it means my night just got a whole lot more interesting."

"I'm glad one of us benefits from this arrangement."

"And there's one more sound I love. Know what that is?"

I hawked a wad of blood-stained spittle onto the floor. "A child's laughter?"

He paused, his eyes sparkling with anticipation. "Better than that, buddy. Listen for it with me now. Hear that?" He grandiosely waved his Marlboro toward the ceiling.

I only caught rock music drifting down from the bar, now muted to the same bass notes I'd heard before entering.

Then, the volume of the bass notes increased substantially.

Cancer gasped. "There it is. The house music getting turned up. You know what that means?"

"They're about to start karaoke?"

He stabbed the glowing ember of his cigarette into my left bicep.

"FUCK!" I yelled, the sensation a mix of getting stabbed and electro-cuted at once. A sudden, searing blast that melted away nerve endings to expose new ones in near-instantaneous succession that ended only when the cigarette extinguished itself on my smoldering muscle. I took several deep breaths, feeling a release of endorphins that replaced the agony with exhilaration.

He tossed the extinguished cigarette to the ground, opened the pack of Marlboros, and tilted it to show me what was inside.

"Now I got nine smokes left in here. That's nine questions, but you know what? I got another pack in the office. Hell, I got a whole carton. I can keep this going all night, but I won't have to. You see, putting a smoke out on your arm don't hurt so bad. The rib, that's ten times worse. Your nipple, even worse than that. But you know what'll really get my questions answered?"

I hissed through gritted teeth, "Free bar tab?"

"Nah, pal. The eye. They hate that. Takes a couple guys to hold their head still. The cigarette won't go out until it gets halfway through your eyeball. Now tell me this: you come from across the river?"

"What?"

"Don't play dumb, pal. The Hudson. You here from New Yawk?"

"No."

"What family you working with?"

"I don't work for anyone."

"Look, I don't give a fuck why you came to Jersey and picked a fight. I want to know why you came here, to this joint, and hit the guy you did."

"Trying to impress a cougar at the bar."

"By getting your fucking ass beat to a pulp?"

"I thought I could take him."

"Pal, you're not taking Viggs, and there's not a woman upstairs who would've taken more than three beers to go home with any guy, much less some pretty boy like you, okay? But you won't be getting your dick wet anymore. There's no way your luck is so bad that you came to the capital of organized crime in Jersey, waltzed into a bar run by wise guys, and hit a made man."

Before I could say anything, footsteps pounded down the stairs. One of the bouncers appeared in the doorway.

"All right, boss, no one else got hit but us. Ran the kid's address—only thing that comes up is it's registered under a foster home license."

"Foster kid? Your parents didn't want you, David Rivahs?"

I swallowed. "Hard to imagine, isn't it, Cancer?"

The bouncer rubbed a fat hand across the back of his neck. "There's one more thing, boss. Tanya said he came in here with some Spic with a goatee. Older guy. Said he split when I broke up the fight."

At this, Cancer swung his eyes to mine.

"Well isn't that interesting. Looks like you aren't some lone nutcase after all. Tell me, who was this guy?"

I shook my head. "Sounds like Tanya is shithouse-hammered, because I came here alone."

Cancer looked to the bouncer. "Go bring your buddy down here so we can do the eye."

"You got it, boss." He turned and left.

"Now until he gets back, let's entertain ourselves by trying your rib. Or you could just tell me who you came here with." He pulled another cigarette from the pack, lighting it and blowing a cloud of smoke into my face.

I coughed twice. "I came alone. That's the truth, whether you believe me or not."

"You're a pretty convincing liar."

He took the cigarette from his mouth, turned it in his hand, and pressed the end between two of my left ribs.

"GODDAMMIT! FUCK YOU, FUCK YOU, FUCK YOU!"

Cancer pressed harder as I thrashed, trying to swing sideways and kick my legs, which were still taped at the ankles. Nothing worked, and it was, without a doubt, the worst pain I'd ever experienced. I shook madly, holding my breath as I tensed until every muscle ached.

For a split second I was back in the basement of the team house—first tied to the chair during Boss's interrogation of me, and then standing across from it watching Luka being tortured.

The ember burned out and I saw Karma on the porch, producing a cigarette for me and saying, *Here, I still owe you one of these.*

When I finally inhaled, the air was putrid with smoke and burning flesh.

Cancer sniffed the air. "Smells like pork, don't it? Not that different from the ribs upstairs."

Footsteps tumbled down the stairs again, and the two huge bouncers reappeared. Cancer looked at them and then nodded in my direction. Without a word, they walked to either side of me as Cancer stepped closer to my face.

Then he spoke calmly, matter-of-factly. "Now listen here, David Rivahs. You can either tell me who you came here with, or you can tell me which eye you want me to burn out first. Your call."

I lifted my chin toward him. "I came here alone, so why don't you pick an eye?"

"Fair enough. I'm gonna go with the right. Hold him tight now, fellas."

The bouncers' hands mashed against my head. My temples, chin, and cheeks were smeared against their thick, sweaty palms.

"FUCK YOU!" I yelled, the words emerging as a muffled roar through the hand covering my mouth. I strained fiercely against their bodies, the handcuffs, whatever I could. Their grip crushed my skull as the glowing, smoldering orb closed in on my face. The smoke stung my eye before the heat did, and I clenched my eyes shut as my lashes began to singe.

"Enough!" a voice shouted from somewhere to my front.

The heat vanished, and I blinked to see Viggs staring back at me in disgust before cutting his eyes to Cancer. "They can hear him upstairs. What's the matter with you?"

Cancer said, "I got him this time, I promise you. He's gonna talk before I get to the second eye."

"Fucking stop it already. He knows we're not going to kill him here. Take him to the harbor and get a drum from out back. If he's going to talk, that's where he'll do it. I'll meet you down there."

He turned and left. Cancer took a drag of his cigarette and shrugged.

"I was wrong about you, David Rivahs. Looks like you'll be getting your dick wet tonight after all."

One of the bouncers pulled a burlap bag over my head, blocking the light from view.

* * *

By the time the car stopped, I was nearly hypothermic.

They had cuffed my hands behind my back, left my ankles tied, and thrown me in the trunk still clad only in pants and shoes. The ensuing drive took the better part of half an hour that may as well have been spent in a meat locker. Within minutes, I'd managed to work my legs between the handcuffs, bringing my wrists to my front and taking the duct tape off my ankles. Then I struggled mightily to kick the trunk open without success. Undeterred, I searched for a way to wriggle into the backseat, found none, and began kicking the trunk again to keep warm as much as anything else.

After I began shaking uncontrollably, I periodically rolled onto my exposed cigarette burns so the agonizing pain would distract me from the sheer cold.

When the trunk finally swung open, the whole crew was looking down at me— Viggs, Cancer, and both bouncers. Shivering violently, and with mucus now streaming from my nose, I closed my eyes and began to whimper.

"Jesus," Cancer said, "he's gonna die before we get him in the water."

The bouncers reached in and grabbed my arms, roughly lifting my trembling body and hoisting me upright as the smell of rotting fish and raw sewage hit me. I saw metal shipping containers stacked behind structures supporting tall cranes. Their pylons were suspended over rippling black water that blended into the glowing maze of the distant New York City skyline. That meant I was standing either beside the Hudson River or some bay offshoot of it.

It would be an iconic end to a dark and troubled existence, I thought with a sense of absurd irony. I was about to die next to the same body of water I used to cross from West Point to reach Ma Bell, the antenna I jumped off not to defy death but to taunt it.

As Cancer stepped in front of me, I kicked him in the groin with all of my remaining strength. He fell where he stood, and I managed to place a second kick across the bridge of his nose before Viggs drilled me in the face, his fist a dense brick against my cheekbone.

I sagged into the bouncers' grip as they hoisted me up again for Viggs to deliver a close-range uppercut into my gut. Taking a single wheeze of air, I spat a spray of blood and tried to yell *fuck you*.

I was only able to rasp the first word of that announcement before they all started beating me at once—first Viggs and the bouncers, and then Cancer when he recovered his composure. I crumpled under the onslaught of sloppy blows. I was pressed against the bumper of the car and then pushed onto the freezing ground as I tried to protect my head from absorbing wild kicks.

Viggs barked, "All right, that's good for now."

As soon as the attack stopped, I began involuntarily shivering again. The bitter cold, the countless impacts, and the now-shredded cigarette burns had all blended together into a delirium of agony.

Viggs knelt beside me.

"I appreciate your balls, kid, I really do. But you're about to go into a fifty-five gallon drum with holes cut in the metal and then thrown into this fucking river. If you're lucky, you'll drown before the crabs climb inside and start eating you. Now, if you tell me why you came into that bar, and who was with you, then I'll let you go with an ass-kicking. You have my word."

I sniffled and took another shuddering breath. "All right. I'll talk."

"Stand him up," Viggs said.

The bouncers lifted me once again as I continued shivering.

I watched Cancer walk to my front, this time out of kicking range. "Enjoy your next human ashtray chained to a pipe, you sick fuck," I said. "Viggs, you're a pussy, and go kill yourself. You two bouncers are just fat, expendable extras in this little drama, so I'm not even going to dignify you with—"

A punch to the face silenced me as my train of thought was scattered into pieces within my skull. They threw me to the ground and began tying my ankles back together with a narrow rope.

When they jerked my arms downward by the handcuffs, I was able to land a single hard bite on one of the bouncer's wrists. He recoiled and slapped my head against the ground as the other bouncer made a series of cross-wraps between my ankle and wrist restraints, binding my body into a fixed crouching position.

At this, I was effectively hog-tied and completely fucked. As they rolled the fifty-five gallon steel drum toward me, complete with a few dinner plate-sized holes in the side, just as Viggs had promised, I used what feeling was left in my fingertips to probe for a knot in the rope.

The only other thing I could move was my mouth, so I did.

"I hope you assholes enjoyed this little soirée as much as I did"—they swung the opening of the drum in my direction and began stuffing me in feet-first—"and have fun stealing scrap metal or whatever the fuck the mob actually does in 2008."

As I probed without success for a knot in the rope, they stood the drum upright with me inside. I could hear them pressing the lid shut as Viggs's eyes appeared before one of the holes.

"Do you ever stop talking, kid?" he asked.

"Viggs, you're lucky these two fat fucks took me down, because this kid would have put you in the hospital by now. Hey, Cancer, you out there?"

I determined that wherever the knot in my rope was, I couldn't reach it.

Cancer appeared in front of the hole. "Talk while you still can, David Rivahs. Because you're about to go in the—"

"Finish your thought, you dumb fuck! What were you going to say? Rivers is going in the river? Do you finally feel as stupid as you sound to everyone else? Bouncers! Hey, you two fat bouncers! Before you die in botched quadruple bypass surgeries, make sure you tell everyone at your shithole bar how much of a fucking twat your boss is. Rivers in the river? Not exactly Broadway material, you clichéd Guido mobster fuck."

His face disappeared from view, and I felt the drum being rocked as they looped a wide strap around it from bottom to top. Then I heard a ratchet being tightened as they sealed me inside.

The drum was pushed onto its flank, the clanging metal impact reverberating like a gunshot inside the confined space.

"David," Viggs said sharply, "tell us what we want to know. This is your last chance."

I was hyperventilating now, my words becoming erratic as they floated on ragged breaths. "I'd rather take a bath at the bottom of this river than listen to you idiots make threats any longer, so let's get on with it. And Newark fucking blows."

At my last word, the drum began rolling before it went into freefall with me inside.

I had just enough time to inhale the biggest gulp of air I could manage before hitting the surface.

Freezing water flooded through the holes, so cold that my exposed skin felt like it was melting off the muscle. The jolting shock almost made me exhale every bit of precious air in my lungs, but before I could, the icy liquid had engulfed my head and I began my descent.

I tried to rotate upside down from my current position so I could kick off the lid. But finding there wasn't nearly enough room to do so, I planted my feet on the bottom of the drum and began slamming my shoulder blades against the lid over and over again in an adrenaline-fueled rush to survive.

It didn't budge.

Frantic, I made a final attempt to find a knot in the rope, only realizing after I began that it wouldn't matter as long as the drum remained sealed. Suddenly I lost all feeling in my hands and feet, and the icy numbness spread to successive joints until my limbs were fully immobilized.

I smashed my shoulder blades upward until my strength faded completely. Peering out of a hole in the thin steel, I saw the distant turquoise lights of the port dimming to blackness as the pressure built in my ears.

My lungs began burning every bit as painfully as the cigarettes did when they seared into my flesh. The drum continued sinking as all else faded to blackness. I lost all control of my body, unable to command even the weakest movement to attempt escape.

My head pulsed with the exertion of maintaining life, and I began swallowing dryly to quell a rising lump in my throat. I felt a curious sense of disbelief, not that I was dying—surely I had come to terms with that over the past years of my life—but that I was dying like *this*. And, in those final moments, my life didn't flash before my eyes in a single cosmic flash.

Instead I saw Karma in vivid color, her crystal blue eyes and glowing skin, the pink-streaked blonde hair and the coral shade of her lips. My vision filled with the ornate tapestry of her tattoos, koi fish and cherry blossoms swirling around her face in a psychedelic matrix that soon began darkening.

I was finally getting the end I deserved, not for the million shattered crimes of my existence but for letting Karma and the team die.

When all had gone black, I was transported to one last memory. I was lying in bed with her after my final dinner with the team, the room so dark that I couldn't even make out her face—only the sound of her voice, the warmth of her body, and her whispered words as we lay there together.

After this is over, come back to Savannah with me.

I opened my mouth and felt the horrifying torrent of cold water rush into my lungs.

Then everything stopped—the pain, the inner resistance, the thoughts —and I entered a state of peaceful tranquility at my life's end that was more profoundly comfortable than any moment preceding it.

Relaxed and content, I closed my eyes and slipped into the darkness.

* * *

I walked down the hallway with a grim sense of determination, the fabric of my socks scraping on the rust-colored shag carpet as I approached the voices coming from the living room.

"—the very fine line between revenge and outright murder."

"You know the difference, don't you?"

Turning the corner, I came to a stop in the dim lamplight and watched the back of the recliner, its fabric surface smoothed by decades of use. Beyond it, faces shifted as drama unfolded within the confines of a wood grain television set.

"Honor."

"As defined by whom?"

"The victor."

Taking a breath, I announced, "I'm not doing this anymore."

A hand reached out from the recliner, lifted the glass of whiskey from the end table, and vanished again. I heard the clink of ice cubes before the hand reappeared, setting the glass back down next to the remote control.

Speaking louder this time, I said, "Dad, I'm not doing this anymore."

The Irish-accented voice called back from the recliner, "You're not doing what anymore?"

"Latin. I quit."

"Oh," the voice replied. "The Latin."

The hand appeared again, this time pressing a button on the remote without lifting it. The television screen went silent, the image of a suited actor aiming a revolver from his waist frozen with his mouth open mid-word.

"I see. Why don't you have a seat and tell me about this decision?"

Walking around the recliner, I sank onto the overstuffed couch and shifted to the edge of the cushion. Sitting up straight, I put my hands on my knees and spoke firmly.

"I'm going to be an explorer when I grow up, so I need to learn something that people actually speak. If I have to see a tutor after school, I want it to be for a real language."

My dad nodded thoughtfully, raising his dark eyes to the ceiling as he ran a hand down his cheeks and over his graying beard, sweeping his fingers into a fist at his chin.

This was a good sign. He always combed his beard when he was taking something seriously.

He set his hands on the armrests and shifted his heavyset body to face me.

"So if we change your tutor, what language would you like to learn instead?"

"Spanish, maybe. Or Chinese."

"Both fine and beautiful languages. I think you'd do just splendidly at either one. Do you know the first time I heard Chinese?"

"I'm serious about quitting Latin. You're not going to change my mind with a story this time."

"And that's not what I intend to do, son. But this brings up a fond memory of your mother for me, so if you have a minute I'd like to recall it with you."

I swallowed, listening to the slow, orderly ticks of the grandfather clock in the corner. "Okay."

"This was back in '83, so you were just a wee lad, though we hadn't met you yet. Your mother and I went to Beijing—you see, back then it was very hard to adopt an American child, and we'd been on waiting lists for over a year with no luck. So your mother, bless her heart, decided we would go to China and have a look at adopting a daughter."

I wrinkled my nose. "You wanted a girl? Why?"

"We wanted a child, and your mother's time was running out. It just so happened that there were many more girls for adoption in China than boys. So a daughter it was, or so we thought."

"Well, what happened? Why don't I have a sister?"

His eyebrows leapt as he continued, "An excellent question, that. As I said, your mother and I arrived and neither of us spoke Chinese, did we? So we relied on a translator, this skinny young lad with glasses who looked like he hadn't had a bite to eat in years. But a cheery lad he was, and so off we went to the orphanage. In fact, he was quite enthusiastic to speak for us. But I soon became convinced he was lying."

"Why?"

"Because when we got to the orphanage—everywhere we went, actually —it seemed like everyone was yelling. And here was this young chap translating the jolliest greetings you've ever heard."

"But they were really being mean?"

"So I thought. I listened to this lady at the orphanage speaking like she was barking orders, and when the translator turned around with a goofy smile and told us, 'She said welcome to China,' I thought he was protecting us from something too cruel to hear. You see, the Chinese inflections and tone can sound very stern to a Western ear. But, in fact, the people we met were quite hospitable."

"Then why didn't you get a little girl?"

His gaze dropped to the carpet. "Your mother was pretty far along at that point. You could see the cancer in her eyes, and wigs still looked like wigs back then. I believe they sensed that little girl would be growing up with just a daddy."

"So what? I'm growing up with just a daddy, and I'm fine."

He paused at this, his eyes unfocused. "Now your mother and I returned to America without a child, and we were devastated. A flight that long takes its toll on a healthy person, never mind someone who's sick, and to return empty-handed...I wouldn't have wished it on anyone. We got back to the house, walked through that door, and your mother just broke down. I held her all night while she cried right there on the couch you're sitting on now."

"So what happened?"

"Well eventually we fell asleep, the both of us. And since we'd been up all night, and our jet lag was quite bad, we slept very late into the next morning. In fact, we didn't wake up until the phone rang."

"Who called?"

"The adoption agency. All the way in Roanoke. You see, you had just passed the minimum time in foster care before an unclaimed infant could be put up for adoption."

"And you came and got me?"

"They tried to make us wait for an appointment, but your mother wouldn't have it. She marched straight to the car and put up such a fuss at the agency that they let her in to have a look."

"And that's when I smiled?"

"That's right. You stood up in your crib—you were quite strong from an early age, you see—and you looked right at your mother and smiled. The biggest smile you've ever seen on a child of any age. And we knew right then and there that you were quite special."

"If I were special I'd have A's in school."

"School's not the measure of a man, son, as you'll grow to learn. That's why I have to teach you on the side, isn't it? The language classes, the target practice, all of it. There are great things ahead for you. I've seen the signs, and when you've been around as long as I have you become an excellent judge of character. Now getting back to my point, if I'd have known how to speak Chinese, that trip to the other side of the world would have been much easier, right?"

"Exactly."

"But let's say we needed to go to Colombia, way down in South America. Well if I went there, the Chinese wouldn't do a lick of good, would it?"

"But Spanish would."

"Yes. If I spoke Spanish, I could get by just fine in Colombia. But what if, from there, I had to travel to the Philippines? They speak Tagalog."

"That's what I'm saying. It's better to know a language that people speak."

"And right you are. But you're an explorer, yes?"

"I will be. When I grow up."

"No, son, you become a thing by being it first. There's no room for wanting—the people who want a thing want it for their whole lives, always dreaming of another day. The doers in this world don't want to be, they *are*. And they *are* in every moment, in every decision, every day of their lives. Now, what are you?"

"I'm an explorer."

"Don't mumble it, boy. Look me in the eye and tell me what you are."

I straightened my back, meeting his stare. "I am an explorer."

"That's the way. You'll become just that to the outside world, because this very night, as an eight-year-old boy who has never traveled outside Virginia, you became it to yourself. And that's how things start in this world —by being, not by wanting."

"I get it now."

He gave a curt nod. "I know you do. Now as an explorer, it would be nice to speak every language in the world. But there are too many. An explorer would much prefer that everyone spoke only one language, but it's not the way things are, is it?"

"If it was, that's what I'd study."

"Now do you know, son, that the source words for half a dozen languages are almost entirely made up of Latin? Why, any language from the warm beaches of Spain, where Christopher Columbus set sail for the New World, all the way to the icy eastern coast of the Soviet Union has its roots in Latin. So it's the only tongue that can give an explorer a distinct advantage wherever he goes—not by knowing how to speak the local tongue but by knowing how to *learn* it. In that regard, Latin is not a dead language but one more alive than any other around the world."

I listened to the continued clucking of the grandfather clock. "Dad, where is Mom?"

He took a sip of his whiskey before setting it back down and looking past me. "Now what do you expect me to say to that?"

"I know she's dead. But where is she now?"

"Son, no one knows what happens after we leave our bodies behind. Anyone who claims to have that wisdom is just stating an opinion. That goes for the cults, too."

"Like those people who keep trying to get us to go to their church?"

"Exactly. Just like those miserable Christians."

"Well, what do you think happens when we die?"

He considered his words.

"If I had to guess, I'd say we go to a place of rest."

"All of us?"

"I think so. But you can come to your own belief, and that's just as good as mine or anyone else's."

"What about the bad people? Do you think they go there, too?"

"Look to nature, son. Is there such a thing as a good or bad animal? Every living thing obeys its instincts and adapts to its environment and circumstances. I don't think humans are any different, and when these Christians come around trying to tell my boy that he was born in a state of eternal sin, I want to hit them in the face, don't I?"

"I guess so." I swallowed. "I'm going to stick with Latin."

"Oh?"

"If it will make me a better explorer."

"I see."

"So I better go back to my room." I slid off the couch.

"All right then, son."

"I'll see you at bedtime, Dad."

"That you shall." He pressed play on the remote control, exchanged it for the glass of whiskey, and took a sip, his eyes on the television as the actor with the revolver continued his monologue.

"*—and if you think that will change my mind, you're going to be sorely disappointed.*"

"*It was worth a shot.*"

"*There's only one shot that should matter to either of us.*"

I walked to the hallway, pausing at the corner to glance at the back of the worn recliner. With his eyes glued to the screen, my dad shifted back to his original position in the seat and called out, "Now go finish your fucking Latin homework."

* * *

My return from death was a howling blur of chaos.

An odd, rhythmic thumping in my chest preceded an explosion of energy, the exhilarating sensation of life immediately crippled by the sheer pain of it all.

I opened my eyes and found myself staring into the sun.

It was pure white, a boundless radiance encompassing everything around me. The profound tranquility of allowing the darkness to take me was replaced by the agony of an existence I didn't want to return to.

I didn't fight for my survival, and I didn't have ethereal sense of meaning; instead, my world was reduced to a moment-by-moment progression of involuntary physiological reactions.

Pinching my eyes shut against the vast, blinding glare, I coughed a huge expulsion of water, then another, and before I could stop myself from inhaling more, I took a surging breath that made my lungs and stomach feel like they were doused in flames.

Karma said, "He's with us now."

I was slammed onto my back, and something soft pressed over my mouth and nose. My lungs filled with burning pain, and I was overcome with the impulse to vomit.

"Here he goes," she said, her voice inexplicably detached. "Turn him."

Hands rolled me roughly onto my side, and the pressure over my mouth vanished. I vomited, feeling the semi-solid, acidic contents of my stomach blanketing my throat.

Karma said, "There's still a lot of peripheral vasoconstriction. Let's get an IV started in the external jugular."

Squinting, I saw figures standing all around me, their faces concealed behind the glow of headlamps. I started to recognize my surroundings, realizing I was back on the harbor when my eyes fixed on an object between two of the people beside me.

It was the steel drum that had entombed me, now resting on its side a few feet away. Then I saw a thin length of cable stretching upward from it, and I followed its length until I could make out a winch connected to one of the metal crane pylons suspended high over the water.

Before I could trace it any further, I threw up again.

They rolled me onto my back, and the seal was pressed over my mouth and nose again as I was gripped by claustrophobia and began thrashing. Hands held me down, keeping my head still. Fingers pulled the skin on my neck taut before a needle was pierced through and then withdrawn, leaving a catheter injecting icy fluid into my bloodstream.

"Core temp?"

"Ninety-two, Doc."

The white headlights blazed down on me as the mask was placed over my face again and my lungs were filled with air, over and over, as the fear gave way to the sensation of freezing to death once more.

"You're safe now. You're doing great. Stay with us."

The voice no longer belonged to Karma but to some unknown woman amid the people around me. My wrists were still handcuffed together, but my legs had been cut loose. I was now stretched flat, restrained against a backboard, taking burning breaths as quickly as I could.

As my senses returned, I realized I was now in motion. The headlights turned in unison as the people around me wheeled my stretcher toward places unknown. I became incoherently terrified that they were about to roll me into the water and began struggling against my restraints with a rising sense of panic.

Instead, I passed into one of the metal shipping containers, its interior as red and warm as a sauna. The figures around me materialized as people in coats and jeans, and I searched their number for Cancer, Viggs, or the bouncers. But the only familiar face belonged to a man waiting inside the container by the time I got there. He approached me calmly, threading his way between the people now attaching round electrodes with gummy adhesive backing onto my chest and ribs.

I began coughing, unable to stifle the impulse. Sergio looked down on me objectively, his dark goatee making his head appear skull-like in the dim red light.

"Congratulations," he said. "You made it to the next round."

Then he turned and walked out, replaced by a young Asian woman with her hair pulled back into a ponytail.

"Try to relax," she said in a clinical tone. "You're being treated by a highly trained medical team that will be monitoring every aspect of your recovery. We'll be raising the temperature in here gradually to let your body adjust, so don't worry if you feel cold. Can you tell me your name?"

I coughed three more times against my will, the catheter in my neck jarring with each convulsion. Finally, I cleared my throat before gasping, "David."

"Last name?"

"Rivers." I coughed again.

"Wonderful, David. And how old are you?"

"Twenty-five."

"Do you know where you are?"

"Unfortunately. Newark."

A pair of hands on the other side of the stretcher began connecting tiny clips to the electrodes, stringing wires across me.

She reassuringly placed the fingertips of one hand atop my shoulder. "You've just undergone a very traumatic experience, and it's perfectly normal to feel frightened. What I need you to do is try and relax, and we're going to make sure your vitals are stabilized before you go into the next round."

"I'll relax as long as the next round doesn't involve being thrown back into the water."

Her lips slid into a smirk. "It doesn't, but you might prefer that. Once we give you an initial medical clearance, you've got an hour to recover before we hand you off to a psychologist. I'm sorry, David, but this is the beginning of a very long night."

* * *

I filled in the final bubble on the stack of papers in front of me, set down the pencil, and leaned back in my chair. Heaving a long sigh, I ran both hands through my short hair that had long since dried in disarray. The medical staff had applied dressings over my cigarette burns, but I could still feel the incredibly tender sores stinging each time I distorted the skin around them by moving in the slightest.

The desk I was sitting behind was located inside a separate shipping container on the harbor and, in stark contrast to the medical supplies in my previous setting, was outfitted with foldout tables stacked with food and beverages. A mass of pizza boxes rested beside a tray of fruit, bottles of water and soft drinks, and a large thermos of coffee. I had been stripped of my soaking wet pants and shoes, and was now wrapped in a bathrobe.

Pushing back my chair, I stood and grabbed an apple from the table and bit into it. I had already eaten a few slices of lukewarm sausage pizza and taken a few sips of coffee since I couldn't stomach the thought of water in any form.

I rapped a fist three times on the metal siding of the wall and yelled, "Doc!"

I had almost finished the apple by the time the psychologist arrived, pulling open the rusty metal door to reveal the day's first sunlight before closing it behind him.

He was an ancient, frail man wearing a giant parka over untold layers of cold weather clothing. His crinkled eyes didn't look at me as he approached the desk and collected the papers from my latest round of testing.

I leaned against the table and took another bite of apple.

"How are you doing?" he asked, still not looking at me.

I swallowed a chunk of fruit. "After four hours of interviews and multiple choice tests, I'm starting to wish I hadn't been resuscitated. Can you bring that Asian doctor back in here? I'm having some really intense chest pain."

He spoke slowly, as if each word were an exertion. At his age, they probably were. "Nice try, David."

I shrugged. "Worth a shot. How did my first tests look?"

"So far, there are a couple outliers of concern."

"Such as?"

"Your results on interpersonal trust are well outside the norm. The scale favors low degrees of trust and forgiveness, but you're below even those. Another issue is your self-confidence."

"Maybe I tested low on trust and confidence because I just got pulled out of the fucking river, Doc."

He turned his head to me and removed his eyeglasses with a withered hand that trembled slightly. "To the contrary, David, your confidence level was on the high side. Ninetieth percentile is a good thing. Ninety-ninth percentile, which *you* are, isn't. Your test scores basically tell us you think you are better than everyone. Most people you meet will, by extension, regard you as somewhat of a"—he considered his choice of words—"cocky asshole."

I shrugged. "Story of my life."

"You deployed once to Afghanistan and once to Iraq?"

"Yes."

"How many people have you killed?"

"Probably more than you."

"How do you feel affected by that?"

"I don't."

"Be honest with me, David. I've worked with many vets, and I know for a fact that you have far more difficulty with sleep, relationships, and feeling any form of human connection to others than you're indicating on your tests. You're underplaying these things with a dexterity that leads me to believe you've been doing so for some time. But such issues have a way of getting worse, not better, the further removed you are from the traumatic experience. Especially when you keep them contained within."

"If I found killing people to be traumatic, I wouldn't be here right now trying to do it again."

"I'm not talking about combat, David. I'm talking about peace."

I blinked hard and saw the psychologist's bulging, ice-blue eyes upon me.

"Doc," I said, smiling, "I appreciate the concern, but I answered your tests honestly. I don't hear voices, I like flowers, and no one ever molested me growing up. I'm ready to get back in the fight."

His shaky hand returned the eyeglasses to his face. He blinked once and looked at me wearily, his stare unbroken. "What do you remember from being dead?"

I hesitated. "What do you mean? There was nothing."

"No light? No emotion?"

"No, I just felt all my resistance ending."

"What else?"

"It was blackness, nothing. The next thing I remember was being revived on the harbor."

"Hmm."

I paused again, strangely bothered by the question. "Why, what do other people say?"

He made a note and flipped his folder shut before sighing with resignation. "I hear everything you can imagine. Lights, tunnels, conversations with dead grandparents, crossing rivers to the far shore...I think, at the end, everyone just sees whatever they believed in."

"But I didn't see anything."

"And that tells me everything I need to know. I think you'll go far in this business, if they let you in."

He turned to leave.

"Wait, what happens next?"

"The medical staff will take you to a hotel. You'll stay there for a couple days while they monitor you for complications from your exposure. Pneumonia, infection, that sort of thing. Once they clear you, you're free to go home."

"Until when?"

"That's not up to me. I'll submit my report, and the rest is their business. If you're selected for an interview, someone will call you. And if you stay in this line of work—alive—then one day I'll see you again."

"I can't wait."

He hesitated. "I've been doing this for a long time, David. You're carrying baggage you can't put down right now, but that doesn't mean you won't be able to unburden yourself one day. So let me offer you a piece of advice."

"I'm listening, Doc."

"A few hours ago, you were dead. Very few people get to change the date on their gravestone once it's been etched. You're here for a reason, son. And you need to remind yourself of that reason every day of your life."

"I'm not sure if you're telling me that this line of work is actually a higher calling, that it's going to do some real good in the world, or if you're telling me to seize this opportunity as a newfound lease on life and get the fuck out while I still can."

"I'm telling you," he replied coldly, "that it doesn't matter which you choose. Because if you don't pick one and hold on to it, it's going to prove fatal very quickly."

"Why? Who's going to kill me if I don't choose either?"

He raised the stack of test papers in his hand, then lowered one corner toward me as if pointing a gun.

"You are, David."

At this, he turned and shuffled away to the other side of the shipping container. Heaving a sigh, he strained to pull open the door as a frigid wind blew past. He tucked his face into his parka and stepped into the morning light, the door slamming shut behind him as he left me alone amid the feast.

REDEMPTION

Fortitudine vincimus

-By endurance we conquer

4

December 17, 2008
Undisclosed Location
Six-hour drive from San Antonio International Airport

I stared at my face in the mirror.

In stark contrast to the state Ian had found me in less than two months earlier, I now looked almost a paragon of credibility. My unflinching deep green eyes were no longer set above the dark semicircles of sleep debt, my pallor was no longer flushed with alcohol and littered with stubble.

The inner truth was much different.

I hadn't yet been assigned my first job in the organization, but the price of admission to date had required me to be beaten, burned, and stuffed first into a trunk and then a steel drum. I had nearly frozen to death before being drowned instead.

My body, already a scarred canvas, was further reflecting the realities of my mind.

I had just received another phone call, followed by a ticket for a red-eye flight to San Antonio, where a driver had been waiting to take me many hours into the desert to an unnamed location I wasn't allowed to ask about. My journey was once more a gravel road leading to nowhere. And yet, just as the shrink had suspected, my face showed perfect professionalism, a veneer of normalcy I could project on demand provided I was sober in the first place.

The mirror stretched from corner to corner in a room long enough to host a full police lineup, the sidewalls each marred by a single door—one to my left leading in, and the other opening to parts unknown.

Everything else was painted a shade of gray that glowed almost white from the long rows of fluorescent lights between the ceiling speakers. In the center of this space, I stood alone for seemingly endless minutes as I waited to be addressed by someone behind the mirror.

Undaunted by the trials I had undergone in New Jersey, my will for revenge held strong.

Karma represented the only savior I recognized, the one salvation I willingly embraced. I had killed her through sheer complacency, through my inability to envision the circumstances of her end, through a list of inadequacies that I didn't want to consider any more than I already had on the sleepless, bourbon-drenched nights of my exile in the Dominican Republic.

I loved her, and the team was the only family I had. Any risk to myself in the process of avenging them was inconsequential by comparison.

My mind quickly corrected itself: I was no longer avenging the team as a whole but whichever two members had been killed by the third.

As this thought occurred to me, the presence behind the mirror spoke at last.

The voice emerged suddenly from the speakers over my head, the words distorted and synthesized into an unrecognizable baritone.

"Let's dispense with the usual formalities. You clearly demonstrated a willingness to die rather than concede failure during your admissions test, so you've earned a chance in the interview room."

I gave a deferential nod. "Thank you, sir. I don't take the opportunity lightly."

"But then I read your psychological evaluation results, and they make me wonder if I should have Sergio executed for recommending you. And trust me, I'm not prone to exaggeration."

"Neither am I. Feel free to elaborate on what you found unsatisfactory."

"First I need to clarify some points on your personal background. You were abandoned at birth and raised by a father whose past—do you know who he really was, David?"

I tilted my head to the side, feeling my neck pop. "Yes. I know."

"Then we can skip ahead to your failed engagement to Sarah Somersby. Together for eight years, only to part ways nine months before the wedding."

"I remember. I was there."

"The timing suggests she wasn't ready to settle down after all."

"Apparently my best friend's dick had that effect on her."

"A betrayal, then."

"Good guess."

"I'll bet betrayal has been on your mind a lot lately, hasn't it, David?"

A lump formed in my throat. Was the survivor behind the mirror?

Before I could consider this possibility further, the voice continued, "Two deployments and then you were off to West Point, from which you emerged single and jobless to spend—am I reading this correctly?—two months hiking in the Smoky Mountains?"

"Something like that."

"That's a long time to spend wandering in the woods."

"Then you fuckers should have called sooner."

A pause. "Now on to the high points of your psychological evaluation. Let's start with the diagnosis of pronounced posttraumatic stress."

I spoke through my teeth. "Why bother?"

"Don't dismiss a clinical diagnosis that came about as a result of your symptoms."

"PTSD is a bullshit medical term coined by people who wouldn't be able to function in a gunfight. The way I am keeps me alive in combat, so the problem isn't with my symptoms, it's with my setting."

"What is it about war that you are finding particularly stressful in the aftermath?"

"The only stressful thing about war *is* the aftermath," I said, feeling my face growing hot. "Put me back in combat and you'll see the most functional human being you've ever met."

"Your evaluation indicated a propensity to interpret instructions. This isn't the line of work for someone who second-guesses orders."

This statement made my brain scramble.

Hadn't Boss said those same words when we were seated around the oak dining table in the team house after I had killed Saamir? I was certain he had, though, in that instant, in that room, I couldn't decide if it was a coincidence, if I had misheard the voice, or if I was losing my mind.

I merely said, "I follow the orders I'm given, without exception. Maybe the shrink thought otherwise because he's turning 120 next week."

"He also said you have an aversion to routine and predictable environments."

"I'm guessing that's preferable to an aversion to stress and uncertainty in this line of work you speak of. And probably a lot less common."

"Perhaps, but if the list in front of me reflects what the psychologist diagnosed despite your best attempts at concealment, I'm left to wonder what secrets you are hiding from us."

I threw my hands up. "Did I miss something? Are you guys looking to hire a kindergarten teacher? If you want a fighter, then I'm your guy, plain and simple. If you want to sit here and talk about feelings through a mirror, then get the shrink to shuffle in here with his catheter bag, because he's a better candidate than I am."

"Then you would have me believe he was wrong about you suffering from depression?"

Weighing my words carefully, I replied, "I don't suffer from it. I'd say we coexist. And I don't see why that matters for the current employment opportunity."

"It matters because we're not running a depression rehab center."

Now I was certain I hadn't misheard. Matz had uttered those exact words when trying to convince Boss and Ophie not to accept me onto the team.

I opened my mouth to respond, but no sound escaped. Instead, a chill of goose bumps swept up my spine onto my neck, and the face in the mirror became flushed, nostrils widening with quickened breaths.

I swallowed, trying to slow my breathing and return my expression to normalcy.

"Anytime you're ready to provide a response, Suicide."

No one but Matz had ever called me Suicide. Not before, not since. I knew in that instant that he stood behind the mirror.

I said, "I've never had thoughts of suicide while in combat, so it won't affect my suitability for employment by an organization that kills people on a regular basis."

"We are bringing in one person for the current assignment, and one person only. No one who has ever done this job has felt prepared for it, but everyone else I've spoken to has a lot more experience than you."

Now I was hearing Ophie, his words quoted verbatim from the meeting after I killed Saamir.

I replied, "Experience and potential are two very different things. And if you can find someone with more potential than me, then I'd like to meet him."

The voice continued, "Regardless, your military experience is insubstantial given what we do. You just don't have the background we're looking for, and given your medical condition, you never will."

That line was Boss's, no doubt—but he couldn't have been alive. Out of all three men, Boss was the one whose innocence had remained absolute in my mind.

I sighed and tilted my head upward. If one of my three teammates was behind the mirror repeating statements that only we would know, then I may as well return the favor.

Swallowing dryly, I said, "You'll find lots of ex-military guys who have flirted with death, but I'm the only one who has married her. And I think you know that already."

"Do I?"

"And you know more about me than that. What you choose to do with that information is up to you."

After a long pause, the synthesized voice spoke once more. "David, I think you and I should meet face-to-face."

"I couldn't agree more."

Silence ensued, the void filled by an unsettling thought that suddenly emerged onto the landscape of my consciousness.

What if all three of my teammates were alive?

It was just as feasible as a single survivor, given the Midnight call that Ian and I both heard in the fleeting seconds before Karma was shot. What if the whole attack on the ambush team's vehicle was fabricated to—

The door handle to my right began to rotate.

I turned toward the noise, never before feeling so vulnerable at the lack of a weapon at hand. But when the door swung open, I felt I wouldn't be able to move if doing so meant saving my life. As we locked eyes, I felt my breath become trapped in my throat, unable to pass in or out.

I wasn't prepared for my interrogator to be someone I'd never seen before.

He was black, with the hulking stature of an amateur bodybuilder. His head was clean-shaven, though his face bore a few days of beard growth. He had hazel eyes, a contrastingly delicate nose, and an easy smile that was spread broadly.

"David," he said, "congratulations. I'll be your partner for the next job. My name is Jais."

* * *

As I followed Jais down a whitewashed hallway leading away from the interview room, I couldn't reconcile the reality of my situation with the certainty I had felt while standing before the mirror. I half-expected Boss or Matz or Ophie to emerge at any moment, and possibly all three at once. In the absence of that, I thought Jais would surely confront me with his knowledge that I was there to kill the Handler, that I was, in fact, a would-be assassin carefully planted by Ian with the complicity of the Indian.

Instead, Jais asked, "Did you get lunch yet?"

"No."

"Me neither. We'll grab something to eat right after I give you a brief overview of our op. You've probably got some questions."

I picked up my pace to remain alongside him. "Where we are right now seems like a good place to start."

"You flew into San Antonio, right?"

"Before sunrise. Where they took me from there, I have no idea."

"We call this the Complex. I'll show you around outside after lunch, but this is ground zero for all operations conducted by the Outfit. Everything we need is right here: an airstrip, a bunch of outdoor ranges, and building mock-ups for rehearsals."

We came to a stop before a closed door, and he turned to face me. "No one gets past here until they get selected for their first job. Some guys go through three or four interviews before that happens."

He took a card from his pocket and swiped it against a gray panel mounted on the wall. The door responded with a hollow click, and he pushed it open before we passed into another hall with a row of doors. Everything looked identical to the last hallway, and every inch of wall space was completely barren.

I said, "Same interior decorator as the rest of the building?"

He kept walking. I followed, the door slamming shut behind us. Jais continued, "Each of these doors goes to a planning bay. You'll be assigned to one of the bays for each job, and no one is allowed in except the people on that particular mission. Once the job is done, the room is sterilized of planning materials and opened for whoever needs it next. There are eight planning bays along this hallway, and we'll be working out of Bay Six."

We came to a stop before a door marked by a plain black number six, and he swiped his badge against another gray panel on the wall. The door clicked, and he opened it to let me in.

When I stepped inside, the lights blinked on automatically.

Jais closed the door behind us. "This is home for the next week."

The room was utilitarian in every sense of the word, with brightly lit white walls reminiscent of a hospital. The centerpiece was a U-shaped semicircle of foldout tables topped with closed laptop computers, their power and connectivity cords ending in an accumulation of bundled cables running to a cabinet in the corner. Rolling office chairs ringed the table assembly, which faced a series of sliding chalkboards with dusty surfaces that had been wiped blank.

A table in the corner supported a coffeemaker and a pyramid arrangement of inverted coffee mugs. Beside them, a bookshelf punctuated the wall between two open doorways.

He said, "Latrine and showers are to the left, sleeping area is through the door on the right."

"Guess I won't be getting lost."

"If you do, I'm going to be sorely disappointed. Have a seat."

I picked a chair at the center of the U, rolling it back and sitting as Jais rounded the tables to stand in front of the chalkboard. Despite his staggering frame, he moved with a lightness and ease that gave the impression of superior athleticism.

As he faced me, the definition of his deltoids created an imposing silhouette against the closed chalkboards. "Our mission," he said, "is to recover a case and return it safely to this facility. We aren't to open the case or attempt to check the contents in any way, only to take possession of what we're given. It is smaller than a briefcase and able to be carried by hand, and I don't know what's inside it so don't bother asking."

"I don't give a shit if it's full of gummy bears. Who has it now?"

"It is currently in transit to a contact we know as the Silver Widow."

I said, "A bit dramatic as far as aliases go. Who is she?"

"Some old crone. And I mean *old* old. Rumor has it she can't even speak any longer. But her relationship to our employer is a sacred one, and we have been instructed to treat her with the utmost respect. No one knows exactly where she is, so we're playing by her rules, and unless we comply with them, we'll never see the case much less bring it back."

"What's her approximate location?"

Jais answered by way of turning toward the chalkboard and sliding two of its panels apart to reveal a huge map depicting the jagged outline of a country I recognized at once.

I said, "We're going to Somalia."

"No," he answered. "We're going to the Wild West. In the next week, you'll learn more than you ever wanted to know about that country. But, for now, trust me that it's a failed state in every sense of the word. The closest thing to order they've had in the past seventeen years is the Transitional Federal Government, which only maintains control over a few areas in the southern half of the country—where we'll be going. A relatively new Islamic group named al-Shabaab has captured most of the rest of the country, with the exception of the capital city of Mogadishu. And they're not that far away from seizing that too."

"To think I was worried about the situation being complicated."

He drew a long breath, holding it for a second before releasing an exasperated chuckle. "You haven't heard the half of it. Depending on the day of the week, you've got government forces that may be trying to maintain control on behalf of the state, acting on decrees from their tribal clan, or just raping and murdering for the hell of it. Then there are African Union troops from half a dozen nations roaming the countryside and US military airstrikes being launched against Al Qaeda from a naval group off the coast. It's total chaos, and that's the easy part."

"What's the hard part?"

"There are various other organizations, both governmental and criminal, that know the case we're seeking is in Somalia. They're searching for it and, of more significance to us, watching all avenues into the country for someone to come and recover it."

I frowned. "Then how are we getting in?"

"You tell me, David. How *are* we getting in?"

I thought for a moment. "The situation sounds too unstable for us to use a ratline without compromising ourselves or the cargo."

"That's an understatement."

"So I'm going to say we get dropped off at night by helicopter."

He shook his head. "The militias out there have extensive early-warning networks. Once a helicopter crosses into their territory, spotters will call in its movement and send patrols if it lands. If that happens, we're dead before we begin. Then you've got airport spotters cross-checking all departing flights against the flight plans, so any aircraft taking off unannounced will be reported—which is fine for getting out of the country once we've got the case in hand, but not before that. Try again."

"If a helicopter's out, then we're going to have to jump."

"Very good. And this particular jump will be the most interesting one of your life."

My mind reversed course to a warm night six months earlier, when I had soared off the roof of Saamir's building in Chicago, my panicked escape from the guard force's bullets sending me into a wild freefall toward the fire trucks and emergency vehicles parked less than four hundred feet below me.

I glanced at the ceiling and then back at him. "That's a bold statement."

"Ever skydived from a commercial airliner before?"

I leaned forward, setting my arms atop the table. "No, but you have my undivided attention."

"So the state-sponsored airline collapsed back in the '90s. Private firms have filled the void, and one of them flies the route from Nairobi, Kenya into Mogadishu, Somalia. We'll be boarding in Nairobi and jumping about halfway through the flight."

He pointed at Nairobi on the map and traced his finger eastward across the border, stopping at a river that bisected the map vertically. "This is the Jubba River, which runs all the way south to the Indian Ocean. Our flight path crosses it near the town of Dujuma, and twenty miles east of that is our exit point and landing zone."

"So the pilots are on the payroll?"

"Absolutely not—the organization has its own aircraft and enough fist-fuls of cash to bribe foreign pilots, but with the whole world looking for the case, we can't count on the usual methods going undetected. This infiltration needs to be something no one will expect, so we'll be hidden in a scheduled shipping container. The pilots won't even know we're on board. So, tell me, how do we exit unnoticed?"

"We don't."

"I'll give you a hint: this is a cargo bird, not a passenger plane. Use your head, David."

Before considering my response, I replied, "I've got seven hundred skydives, and I am using my head. You can't open the door of a commercial airliner in-flight due to air pressure, so we'd have to use explosives. That alone would cause a catastrophic decompression that we probably wouldn't survive. Even if we're equipped for the lack of oxygen and freezing tempera-tures at high altitude, we'd still be exiting while the plane is flying at a cruising speed fast enough to kill us instantly. And if we miraculously made it through all these factors, the ensuing investigation is going to uncover a shipping container outfitted for two jumpers that remained in the cargo bay. No matter what, we're not exiting unnoticed."

Jais folded his arms, watching me with a detached expression and tilting his head slightly. "The shipping container will be filled with humani-tarian supplies, and we'll get kitted up for the jump in Nairobi before getting in the box. There will be no evidence remaining of us having been inside."

"That doesn't help all the other factors I just brought up."

"Then maybe this will. The aircraft is a DC-9-30, which is a twin-engine bird. Everything behind the cockpit is a Class E cargo space, meaning it's inaccessible by the pilots while in flight and has no fire retardant measures. So as we approach Dujuma, we're going to set off the smoke detectors in the back. Since the pilots can't physically check what's wrong, their standard procedure is donning their oxygen masks, depressurizing the aircraft to cut oxygen supply to the fire, and descending to thirteen thousand feet so they can breathe after their on-board air supply runs out."

"We'd still need to use explosives to exit."

"You're right about that part. I'll be detonating a small explosive charge to knock out the tail door. We'll jump through that."

"Then the airline investigation is going to figure out what happened."

He held up an index and middle finger. "Mitigated by two factors. First, there is going to be a public claim of responsibility for blowing up the plane, ostensibly released by al-Shabaab on the night of our jump. The group has plenty of motivation to disrupt an aid flight on its way to government control, and it has expanded so rapidly in the past year that the leadership won't be able to confirm or deny that one of its cells or their sympathizers carried out the attack."

"And the other factor?"

"The airline itself is going to prevent outside investigators from gathering forensic evidence. They're going to conclude it was a failed terrorist attack and continue with business as usual."

"Why would they stop an outside investigation?"

"Why do you think?"

I thought for a moment. "The only reason I could see is that it's a dirty flight to begin with, and they wouldn't want anyone poking around the contents of the plane."

"Yes and no. Our plane *will* have legitimate aid on its way to the Transitional Federal Government—that's no accident, since it has to appear that al-Shabaab has an incentive to blow it up. But the same airline facilitates a lucrative smuggling racket that funnels arms to the Somali militias, funded by wealthy supporters in the Middle East. The airline's leadership would be on the blacklist of a lot of very bad people if they allow outside scrutiny of their operations."

"Okay, I get it. Now, this whole thing sounds really—"

"Crazy? Trust me, I've done the research, and we've confirmed the airline's emergency procedures and their policy of covering up any incidents that would draw attention to undeclared cargo. It'll work."

"I was going to say brilliant, not crazy."

He uncrossed his arms and nodded appreciatively. "I know, right? And since the plane already will have undergone a controlled depressurization, the explosive charge will just create some structural instability. The pilots aren't going to execute an emergency landing over Indian country, so they'll make it all the way to Mogadishu. That leaves no crash site for everyone in the area to try and exploit for supplies or propaganda, which means you and I arrive in Somalia undetected."

I drew a long breath, turning my gaze from Jais to the map. "What's the landing zone like?"

"Easy money. It's all open desert out there, so all we'll see is a set of infrared strobes set up by the reception party. After we link up with them, we'll turn over our weapons and GPS and get blindfolded. Only they can take us to the Silver Widow, because she won't divulge her location to the Outfit. We take control of the case, get blindfolded again, and then they'll transport us to the foothills outside Saakow, about thirty miles north of our landing zone. From there, a helicopter will arrive and take us east to Mogadishu."

Nodding slowly, I said, "If they're taking us to the helicopter, why not just trade the case at that point?"

"They've refused that option already. In fact, they won't even come within two miles of our pick-up site in case our helicopter shows up early— they're dropping us off, and we have to walk there. Once the helicopter arrives, it takes us straight to the Mogadishu airport. We'll board a jet back to San Antonio and then take a small plane to the Complex airstrip right out back so we can hand over the case. And that's mission complete."

"Why did you call me Suicide in the interview?"

He hesitated, watching me coldly. "Don't ask me anything related to your interview ever again. As of right now, that topic is officially off-limits. When you're standing on the other side of the glass, you'll understand."

"Then I've got another stupid question for you."

At this, I saw a flash of anger cross his face. "But you're going to ask it anyway."

"This mission seems pretty straightforward for one person to carry out. Why do you even need a partner?"

Jais's features softened. He walked to the corner of the U-shaped table formation and pulled out a rolling chair next to the coffeemaker. Lowering himself into it, he lifted one ankle onto the table, then the other, and leaned back with precision, both hands behind his shaved head.

His hazel eyes watched me patiently. "Two men are always better than one when going into the badlands. And the case is heavy, probably forty or fifty pounds of dead weight. As I said, we have a two-mile walk uphill to our pick-up point. That means one man on point and another hauling the load. So, the truth is, I don't need a partner. I need a mule. And that's a perfect assignment to break in a new guy."

"I'm guessing you were military before this?"

"Among other things."

"Such as?"

"I used to work on a private paramilitary team, the kind of guys this organization would outsource work to."

I felt a rush of excitement and tried to sound casual as I asked, "Do a lot of guys from those teams come work here?"

He shook his head. "I don't know everyone who works out of this place, but I know most of them. And besides me, I've never seen any cross-pollination between the outsourced teams and the Outfit."

That meant one or more of my teammates could still be alive, albeit outside Jais's purview. But if that were true, then how could he have spoken those particular words in the interview?

I asked banally, "What's the difference between those teams and the Outfit?"

"Anything that can be outsourced to a freelance group, is. The people who work out of the Complex handle whatever jobs are deemed too vital to the organization's interests to use outsiders."

"Deemed vital by whom?"

"People above our pay grade. All you need to know for now is the work you signed up for is unique. It requires either safeguarded organizational methods or very sensitive material."

"Which one is the mission we're about to do?"

He lifted his chin, directing his eyes to the ceiling, his expression empty.

"Trust me, David, when I say that this mission is both."

5

December 25, 2008
The Complex

"We're not beating the rain out of here," I said to Jais, who was seated on the tailgate beside me.

From our vantage point, our backs turned to the pickup bed loaded with our equipment bags as the truck rumbled forward, we watched the bone-white walls of the Complex buildings receding under a swath of mid-morning storm clouds stretching toward us, threatening to unleash a flood at any moment. The tall dirt berms punctuating outdoor shooting ranges appeared in the periphery and likewise swept to our rear, interspersed with the high metal roofs of multi-level buildings for practicing urban combat with live ammunition.

Jais made a disappointed ticking sound with his tongue. "Such a pessimist. We'll be well on our way to San Antonio before the first drop."

"God forbid they pair us together again after this, because you can't tell weather worth shit. After two dozen freefalls together, I was starting to like you, but now you've crossed a line."

He didn't respond, and I looked over to see his easy smile fading into a faraway look.

"What's wrong?" I asked.

He hesitated. "After Somalia, we'll never see each other again."

"Why not?"

"This is the last mission before my meeting."

"What meeting?"

"With him, David." His smile returned, but this wasn't the easygoing, confident look I'd become so familiar with over the past week. This time, his face assumed an expression of dreamlike hopefulness that looked totally alien on him.

I said, "You've never mentioned him. Who is he?"

"Here at the Complex, we call him the Handler. But after I deliver on this mission, I will call him the One."

"I thought you were never going to speak of him, this guy. The One."

"Unless you're chosen to meet him, he's known as the Handler."

"Handler. The One. Whatever. How many get chosen to meet him?"

"Very few. It's a great honor. Most of the senior operators here have never seen his face and never will. Hell, Sergio's been here longer than most and he'll never be granted an audience."

"Well how did you end up being so fucking special?"

He said nothing as the truck braked to a stop. I heard the metallic rumble of the sliding gate opening behind us. We pulled forward into the fence-lined space, stopping again before the second gate. The first gate, composed of the same chain link privacy fence that lined the entire complex, slid shut in front of us. The gate's metal weave was threaded with brown slats that erased the Complex from view as it clicked into place.

Only then did we hear the next gate rattling open, and the pickup pulled forward to reveal the vehicle search area known as the lock-out chamber. Metal poles ending in slanted mirrors used for searching vehicle undersides were leaned against the fence beside the working dog kennel, and three guards with weapons slung across their chests—two assault rifles and a shotgun—milled about in conversation. The entire scene disappeared as the second gate veiled its presence and our pickup rolled forward past the outer fence that stretched brown and limitless to both sides.

Once the guards were well out of earshot, Jais said, "I got my invitation just before your interview, but I've been getting groomed for a while now.

Tougher missions, more responsibility. He sees everything, and he liked what he saw out of me."

"I thought this was an easy mission."

"It is."

"Then why is he using his golden boy to lead it?"

"The hardest missions aren't always the most important."

I ran my palms down my cheeks, swiping my fingers together across my jawline. "You know exactly what's in the case."

Jais didn't respond, neither speaking nor looking at me as the dusty white walls of the hangar appeared around us. A high ceiling of criss-crossed metal beams blocked the storm clouds as the driver steered a wide circle under a giant American flag suspended high above our heads. Jais and I now faced the large open hangar doors and, beyond that, the airfield stretching to the east under a turbulent sky of cobalt and gray.

The pickup's engine went silent, the final echo vanishing into the distant buzz of an approaching plane before I heard the chirp of its tires on the runway.

"That's us," Jais said.

He hopped off the tailgate. I followed suit, waiting for him to speak again even as I knew he wouldn't. Our driver exited the truck, slamming his door shut behind him as he walked to the opposite side of the hangar where a second pickup sat, its tailgate lowered and bed empty.

Another team must have been returning on the plane that was about to whisk me and Jais to San Antonio, I thought.

Once there, we would load our equipment into a shipping container outfitted with mattresses and sleeping bags for our trip. For the next two legs of our journey—eight and a half hours to London Heathrow and then another trip of equal length to Nairobi—neither of us planned to be awake. We had sleeping pills to force rest on the flights, or as Jais called it, "time traveling."

Any rest we got would end the moment we arrived in Nairobi. There we would don our parachutes, rig our equipment for the jump, and move into a smaller container filled with legitimate aid supplies to be uncovered in the ensuing investigation of a mid-air emergency.

After being loaded into the DC-9-30, we'd wait an hour before taking off on a flight that we'd remain on for less than forty-five minutes before initiating our escape. From landing under parachute, to recovering the case, to our extraction by helicopter, we would be on the ground in Somalia for less than twenty-four hours. The schedule left us no time to rest besides what we could manage as we crossed the Atlantic Ocean.

The prospect seemed less daunting in the wake of Jais's words. *Most of the senior operators here have never seen his face and never will.*

I wasn't even a junior operator yet; hell, I hadn't even embarked on my first mission with the Outfit. How long would it take me to amass Jais's level of seniority? And even he couldn't give me a straight answer on why the Handler granted him a meeting beyond attributing the honor to a vague notion of his master seeing everything.

What was I to do, continue racking up missions for years and hope I eventually fell among the minority who got to meet the Handler? That seemed as effective a strategy as assassinating the president by committing one's lifetime to charitable achievements in the hope of one day getting an invitation to the White House.

Yet my glimpse into the Handler's affairs, coupled with the Indian's nebulous information as our sole source of intelligence, led me to believe that this was apparently the best that Ian and I could do.

My thoughts were interrupted by the appearance of a sleek white plane fuselage rolling into view between the open hangar doors. Its engines slowed to an idle as it stopped, and a rear section of the plane unfolded to expose a row of five stairs that came to rest a foot over the ground.

A man emerged from the plane wearing a plate carrier covered in pouches and carrying an SR-25 rifle with suppressor. His sleeves were rolled to the elbow, and as he turned his sweaty face toward us, I recognized him as Cancer.

The man who had put cigarettes out on my flesh looked to me for only a moment before cutting his eyes to Jais as if I weren't there. He gave a slight shake of his head.

Jais nodded back.

Cancer descended the stairs as another man appeared, his weapon slung over his shoulder and both hands behind him, holding something heavy as he carefully negotiated the narrow staircase. I couldn't make out what he was carrying until the third man appeared a few seconds later, stepping out the door and lifting his arms to keep his cargo off the steps. Suspended between them was a length of shiny black material contoured into a long, familiar shape.

It was a body bag.

Several more men emerged from the plane, hauling equipment bags down the steps to the concrete floor and toward the opposite pickup. The last man in their number waved us toward the aircraft.

Jais grabbed a bag out of the back of our truck, then threw it over his shoulder and hoisted another to carry by hand. "See?" he yelled to me over the plane's engines. "I told you we'd beat the rain."

With that, he turned to the waiting aircraft. After watching him approach it for a few seconds, I grabbed two bags and jogged after him. I slowed as I caught up to him, and together we neared the lowered stairs of the plane, its engines idling as an unseen pilot waited for us to board.

DESCENT

Amicus certus in re incerta cernitur

-A true friend is discerned during an uncertain matter

6

December 28, 2008
29,000 feet over the Kenya-Somalia border

Beyond the orb of our helmet lights loomed only blackness in the cargo area, a frigid, vacuous metal space more comfortable to me than any warmly appointed room of my lifetime.

There was a peculiar harmony to be found amid the rumble of a plane's interior, the white noise of a thousand aircraft flights whose dichotomy was twofold. During travel, its soothing presence eased me to sleep in a way I rarely experienced on solid ground; during a jump, its sudden disappearance proudly heralded the exhilarating rush of freefall.

The sound of the flight was, however, muffled by the radio earmuffs hugging the side of my head, which were attached to a helmet made heavier by the binocular night vision device flipped upward on its rotating mount. Between that and the rubber contour of my oxygen mask forming a seal over the lower half of my face, propelling a steady flow of air into my mouth whenever my lips parted, only my eyes were visible, and even those were shielded by clear goggles tightened snugly over them.

The rest of me was a mass of equipment strapped over cold weather gear, the combined bulk turning Jais and me into waddling marshmallow men unfit for any Hollywood depictions of combat. The parachutes alone were tremendously large, both main and reserve canopies able to bear the weight of a grossly over-equipped jumper. Add to that the inverted combat packs with water, survival rations, first aid supplies, and ammunition, all of which was encapsulated by an intricate H-harness that hung them over our thighs, and the Israeli Galil assault rifles we wore flush against our left sides like a splint from shoulder blade to waist, and we were scarcely able to walk, much less jump.

The coup de grâce was the oxygen bottles mounted in a pouch beneath our rifles. Absent any oxygen panels on the aircraft, we'd needed them to sustain us for an hour of pre-jump breathing to reduce the nitrogen levels in our bloodstream and prevent decompression sickness. The bottles may as well have been bowling balls slung beside our hips and, by virtue of taking all evidence of our presence with us out of the plane, had to be jumped along with everything else.

Adding to our mobility issues was the fact that we wore extreme cold weather gear, a vital consideration in the unheated cargo bay. With a 3.5-degree decrease in temperature for every thousand-foot increase in height, our current altitude put us somewhere around negative twenty-three degrees, cold enough to induce frostbite on unprotected skin even in the short time it took us to exit the plane. Given the added wind chill in freefall, the cold would quickly prove fatal to an unprepared jumper.

I turned my head to orient the circular glow of my helmet light over Jais's gloved hands as he carefully positioned the explosive charge over the rear airstair, which was locked into place by a clamshell door just under the plane's tail.

A sudden jolt knocked me clean off my feet, and I hit the metal floor hard under the weight of my gear, the back of my helmet bouncing sharply.

"You all right?" I called to Jais.

I could see his helmet light beside me on the floor as his distorted voice echoed through my radio earmuffs. *"Yeah. We must be hitting turbulence."*

The plane suddenly plummeted, causing my body to levitate for two long seconds until the floor lurched back toward me and I smashed into it once again. Then the fuselage jolted sideways as if pushed by an invisible hand, stabilizing for just a moment before ascending and pinning us to the ground.

"This feels pretty rough," I said. "Should we bump the timeline?"

I slid sideways and crashed into a crate as he answered, "*If we're still on this plane when it lands in Mogadishu, he'll kill us both.*"

"I thought I was the expendable one, not you."

"*We're both expendable. If we die, he'll send another pair within a day. And another pair after them, and another after them, until he gets what he wants.*"

Our already dangerous infiltration into Somalia was now further complicated by raging winds, and the prospect was thrilling to me. Maybe it was because I wasn't in charge and it wasn't my mission to fail, but above any fear for our personal safety came the simple fact that I liked when things went wrong on a jump.

Nothing was more anticlimactic than a parachute affair that went exactly according to plan, a sure sign that one would sooner or later forget the jump had ever occurred. Any potential at transcending mediocrity would soon be lost amid the same groundswell of monotony that swallowed up everything else in life. When I looked back upon the hundreds of jumps I had done, the ones that stood out were those that, with better judgment or more experience, would never have occurred.

And whatever happened this night over East Africa, I was certain that, if I survived, the jump would be seared into my memory like the cigarette burns on my body, taking its place among the other proud scars of gunfights and combat and missions both good and bad, military and criminal, their sum total just barely making the meaninglessness of life worth enduring.

"Well," I said, "at least this will make for a hell of a story. If we survive it."

Jais's helmet light swung to the GPS on his wrist. "*Goddammit, there must be a storm. They're diverting south off the flight path. Stand by for emergency bailout.*"

I scrambled to my feet, moving as quickly as the bulk of my equipment would allow, and shone my lamp along the interior of the fuselage to locate the smoke detector. Fumbling thickly gloved hands into my pocket, I withdrew the butane lighter and said, "You know, between the storm outside and the cabin fire in here, these poor fuckers flying the plane are about to have the worst night of their lives."

"*Light it! Now!*"

I cracked the lighter into a spike of blue flame, holding it toward the rectangular detector above me. Within seconds, a red dot began blinking rapidly.

"Smoke detector's activated," I said.

No sooner had the words left my mouth than a vast whooshing noise drowned out the droning engines. My ears popped twice, and then over and over in rapid succession.

"*We're depressurizing. Air pressure is fifteen thousand feet... twenty thousand feet... standby for detonation.*"

I checked my wrist. "We're still flying over 180 knots."

"*If we don't jump now, we'll be over the Indian Ocean. Three. Two. One.*"

I breathed the words, "See ya," as a blinding orange glow erupted amid the sharp bark of the explosive charge, illuminating the plane's cabin and then immediately plunging it into near-blackness.

A sharply defined portal glowed an eerie phosphorescent blue as it punctuated the darkness, its edges lined in whistling flame.

I charged toward it, my combat pack bouncing off straining thighs as Jais yelled, "*Go! Now!*"

His helmet light shone to my right beside the missing door, and I extinguished mine a split second before his too went dark. Only the sky's radiance remained. Wind whipped against my helmet as I closed in on the empty doorway—five feet, three—and a hard bounce of turbulence caused me to plunge through it virtually headlong.

My vision became a violent cyclone of dark hues, and I barely glimpsed the plane, now two hundred feet distant, as I was ripped by the undertow of wind into the night sky over Somalia.

I arched my back, trying to stabilize as the combat pack beneath me became a center of gravity around which I twirled in a flat spin, the mask pressing against my face in one direction and the goggles in the other. Twisting my shoulders against the rotation, I began to slow as my mind struggled to fathom how I had been able to see the plane after jumping at night. Bewildered by the flashes of light around me, I wondered if I was losing consciousness.

As my spin slowed, I looked around and saw that I was freefalling between storm clouds of immeasurable height, their undulating columns flickering with bursts of lightning a mile in every direction. The plane must have been threading its way between them as we jumped, and I looked down at a featureless blanket far below me, unsure whether it was the ocean or a base of clouds and realizing there was nothing I could do about my situation in either case. To pull my parachute was to ensure its immediate collapse amid the winds that buffeted me from seemingly every direction at once.

A dark shape descended toward me from above, stopping at eye level with impossible grace, its outline fluctuating with expert adjustment amid the wind.

The next bolt of lightning revealed the shape as Jais, and we connected arms as the sky went darker again, his body now silhouetted only by the blue indigo beyond.

I couldn't believe it—the speed at which we exited was too fast for any jumper, however skilled, to make a linkup mid-air, much less at night while burdened with tactical gear. And yet there he was, clasping my right wrist and I his, just as we had on two dozen practice jumps in the desert outside the Complex.

"No one's going to believe this!" I said into my mask, hearing only garbled static in response.

The green disc of the altimeter on my left hand showed us descending past eleven thousand feet. The flat surface beneath us was much closer than that—clouds, I realized, rather than water. It rushed up to meet us as Jais tightened his hold on my wrist and I did the same to his before a hazy mist obscured my view.

I strained to read my altimeter through the fog and saw the needle descend past six thousand feet just as we passed through the bottom of the clouds. Somalia appeared below us, an endless black void beneath intermittent flickers of lightning.

No sooner had the ground materialized than Jais pulled his hands away from mine, yanked his rip cord assembly, and was plucked from my view by his deploying canopy.

My first thought was that my altimeter was off—we had planned to take it down to 3,500 feet before pulling—until I turned my head to see what he had been looking at as we cleared the clouds.

Behind me was a vast city, a thousand fires burning within the glowing windows of densely packed structures ending in three concave semicircles that marked the coastline.

I immediately pulled my rip cord, and my body jerked upright as I took control of the steering toggles. Frantically glancing behind me, I directed my canopy north, away from the ocean, while aiming for the outskirts of the city. As I lowered my night vision device in front of my eyes, the town appeared in murky shades of green. Gusts of wind blasted my canopy from the left, and I adjusted control inputs to counteract it as my body swung under the risers.

"Jais? Jais?" No distorted voice responded this time, not even static, as I desperately tried to identify a suitable landing area amid the rapidly approaching ground. The buildings were spread farther apart as I flew northward, but for every surge of forward momentum came a headwind that pushed me back or a crosswind that rocked my parachute sideways.

I dared not release my combat pack to dangle on its lowering line, fearing the volatile winds would turn it into a pendulum that would further complicate an already bad situation. Instead I chose to ride it into the ground, passing over a walled compound before pulling my toggles down to bleed off altitude. I descended into an open patch between buildings, flaring as much as possible in a hard, rolling landing right into a slick of mud.

What followed was a frantic rush to strip off my gloves and parachute in a desperate bid to free my assault rifle from its rigged configuration at my side. I tore at the quick-release folds in canvas straps, pawed at metal buckles, and writhed in a series of contortionist maneuvers while trying to remain prone and avoid detection.

Somewhere in this process, I heard a rippling flutter growing in volume over the wind and swung my night vision upward to see Jais descending under canopy to a running landing twenty-five meters away.

The rain had stopped, and a low growl of thunder rolled across the clouds as I finished stripping off my equipment. A necessary inconvenience in the aircraft, the cold weather clothing had become a sweltering death trap amid the sea-level air.

By the time I made it over to Jais, my own parachute stuffed into a kit bag now resting over my combat pack, his rifle was on the ground at his side while he gathered his canopy.

I took a knee a few feet away to provide security, scanning the green landscape of low rooftops and compound walls, looking for movement but seeing none.

I whispered, "We're in Kismayo, aren't we? Pretty much the al-Shabaab capital?"

"Yup," he replied, continuing to bundle his chute.

"If my grasp of Somali geography is right, and I'd like to think that it is, we're about a hundred miles southwest of our landing zone."

"At least a hundred."

I heaved an exasperated sigh. "Well, at least it's better than landing in the ocean, right?"

He shoved his parachute harness into the kit bag and then slung his combat pack over his shoulders. "That depends on whether or not we can find a car."

* * *

Through my night vision, the landscape around us was an eerily familiar convergence of translucent emerald shapes marking primitive construction. Dirt roads and alleys collided and parted in a skewed mishmash that had evolved from footpaths over hundreds of years. The building density fluctuated without rhyme or reason as the outskirts of the city unfolded.

It just as easily could have been a dozen towns I had patrolled in Afghanistan, with the exception of the sporadic trees and power lines overhanging narrow streets. And while the night air was saturated with fresh rainfall, I knew what scents the next day's scorching sun would bring: the residue of dust and livestock, sand and feces both animal and human, the smells of prehistory that had remained intact amid the world's undeveloped and forgotten corners.

Jais and I walked toward the main road leading north out of town as sheets of fading rain came and went. I scanned for movement only to find that the passing storm was now, and only now, working to our advantage by keeping the population indoors. Stray dogs betrayed our presence, darting between buildings in scattered packs and barking noncommittally before melding into the shadows.

We had both taken the time to strip our cold weather gear and transfer our night vision devices to lightweight head mounts, but we still had to tote the kit bags holding our jump gear that made any progress on foot a burdensome endeavor.

When Jais rounded the corner of a building and stopped in his tracks before kneeling and peering around to the right, I knew he'd found what we were looking for.

I approached and kneeled beside him, peeking at an old Hilux pickup parked beside a long, single-story structure.

He whispered, "Cover me while I boost it."

I crossed to the opposite side of the intersection and set down my parachute kit bag, then knelt at the corner of the building to look down the street beyond the vehicle. Jais was now placing his kit bag and combat pack into the bed of the truck.

Then he smashed his rifle's buttstock into the driver's side window, and I heard the faint crunch of glass before he opened the door and disappeared inside. As I scanned the streets to provide cover for Jais while he hotwired the vehicle, my thoughts turned to my interview for the job that we were now trying to salvage from the ashes of a chance weather event.

I had unquestionably heard the words of my former teammates in the interview room, near-verbatim quotes from a single meeting the day after I killed Saamir. Those words were spoken by a synthesized voice that I couldn't conclusively identify, and while Jais had been the one to appear from behind the mirror, he hadn't used that same language since then.

I felt confident he hadn't been the one to interview me, lending further credence to my belief that either Boss, Matz, or Ophie had survived and was watching unseen yet allowing me to live. Only the team would have known what was said that day—no one else was present. Yet I began to feel an inexplicable, nagging suspicion that there was someone else I wasn't considering.

As my thoughts marched toward the next corner of rumination, I heard the truck engine fire to life.

The pickup drove forward and stopped beside me. I grabbed the handles of my parachute kit bag in one hand, rose, and tossed it into the bed before trotting to the passenger side.

Opening the door, I unslung my combat pack and set it between my legs as I slid onto the cloth seat. I rested my rifle next to the pack and eased the door shut as Jais pulled forward, accelerating down the muddy street without headlights.

Erasing the interview from my mind, I said, "Well, this is off to a promising start."

Jais drove from an awkward position, working a stick shift while holding his head high. His mouth was partly open as he tried to angle his night vision binoculars toward the windshield at the best angle. "Buttery smooth all around," he said. "Basically, everything to our south and east is ocean, and we couldn't be farther from safe territory, which is either the government-controlled region near Mogadishu or across the Kenyan border in the opposite direction. And this truck only has a quarter tank of gas."

"We've got the satellite phone. You could call in the helicopter."

He shook his head. "I'll use the phone to send a report, but that's it. If I call to request a bailout before we get the case, the Outfit won't forgive us."

"We landed a hundred miles off target due to factors completely outside our control," I insisted. "Most would consider this an emergency, if not an outright goddamn catastrophe. I think requesting a little assistance is understandable."

"You're wrong. They'd send shooters on the bird to make sure we paid for quitting on them and then leave our bodies for the enemy or the hyenas, whichever came first."

"Lovely. So what do you want to do?"

"You've got a map, David. You tell me."

"This isn't the time for the Socratic method, Jais."

"I disagree completely. Let's see how you handle pressure." Jais turned left onto the first road heading north out of Kismayo.

I pulled the waterproof map case from my cargo pocket and unfolded it in my lap as I flipped my night vision device upward on its mount. I turned on a red light, holding the lens just over the map's surface.

I checked my GPS and began examining the map. "The road we're on heads northeast along the coast for about ten miles until it hits the village of Goobweyn at the outlet of the Jubba. Then the road turns north along the river—we're on the wrong side of that, by the way—and we've got another sixty miles to the first bridge at Jilib before we can cross to the east side of the Jubba and keep moving toward the landing zone."

"That bridge is going to be under the control of one militia or another, guaranteed. And we're not making it across with your milky complexion."

"A little racist, but I'll concede that profiling is more widely accepted here than it is back home. Perhaps you'd prefer to play swim roulette through the hippos and crocs living in the Jubba?"

"It's your plan now, David. Is that what you want us to do?"

"I'd prefer to trade this car for a boat in Goobweyn."

"What makes you think we can find a boat there?"

"If the town's at the outlet of the Jubba, its economy will rely at least partially on open water fishing. No one's going to interfere with that as long as al-Shabaab or whatever militia is in charge gets their cut."

"Good, David. What next?"

I slid my red light across the map. "So we'll ride the river and stop short of Jilib, drag our boat into the jungle and wait until nightfall, and then continue under night vision under the bridge and all the way up to Dujuma. We can find a car there before daybreak tomorrow and drive twenty miles east across the desert to our landing zone."

Looking over, I saw him nodding in approval. "That's the ticket. Traveling by river will be a lot faster than driving along these shit roads, and once we hit contested territory we'd be running into militia checkpoints anyway."

"Will the reception party still be at the landing zone by the time we make it there?"

"The Outfit will be able to relay our updates, but we're well outside the terms of the agreement. Whether the reception party chooses to come find us or not doesn't really matter—we've got no other options."

I rotated my night vision back down as Jais piloted the vehicle forward into the night. The muddy road extended endlessly to our front, appearing now in muddled hues of green, and neither of us spoke again for a long time after that.

* * *

We neared Goobweyn shortly after six in the morning, the sky finally brightening above us. While we'd taken advantage of the drive to eat and restore our strength as much as possible, after a long, sleepless night there was a certain rejuvenation that could only be achieved upon seeing the sunrise.

Unfortunately, the daylight forced me to take the demeaning measure of donning my *shemagh*.

Jais said nothing as I fished out the balled mass of black and white patterned cloth from my pack, but I knew a droll comment was coming as I struggled to arrange the cotton material into the folds I'd practiced back at the Complex. He waited until I had covered the top of my head and was wrapping the excess fabric sideways across the lower half of my face before speaking.

"Yeah," his deep, melodic voice sang from behind the wheel, "put on that rag of obedience."

With my voice muffled by cloth, I said, "Jais, you're built like a fucking linebacker. Don't act like you're going to blend in any better."

"I'll blend in better than you, cracker."

I finished tying the corners together behind my head. "Whatever. How do I look?"

He glanced at me and then turned his eyes back to the dirt road, shaking his head. "I don't know what the fuck you look like, David. Some kind of suburban terrorist wannabe, I guess."

He was dressed as I was, in lightweight civilian clothes offset by an olive green canvas chest rig holding three AK magazines with grenade pouches to spare. We had chosen Israeli Galil assault rifles for their ability to reliably fire under the filthiest of conditions and, more importantly, to accept standard AK-47 magazines and 7.62 x 39mm ammunition. One could find these in abundance anywhere in the Third World.

I looked out the passenger window at the occasionally visible sliver of ocean along the horizon and saw it had disappeared altogether amid a broad, rolling expanse of hard-packed red dirt and scrub brush. Jais steered our truck through a bumpy right turn off the main road and onto a trail marked by little more than a set of tire tracks. Thatch and sheet metal roofs were visible through the trees to our left.

Jais said, "I'll park by the water and walk along the river until I find the closest thing they've got to a speedboat. Stay with the truck, and don't come after me unless you hear gunshots."

"You've got to be kidding. It's suicide to walk in there alone."

"A bit farther north and I'd agree with you. But we're ten miles outside Kismayo—this isn't contested territory, the locals have survived this long, and I've got a two-inch stack of Somali shillings in my pocket that speaks louder than another guy with a rifle will."

"All the more reason I should be there to back you up."

"If you get close and they see you're white, what are they going to think? They've had US fighters and drones flying overhead for years now. I can keep my mouth shut and give them some cash without issue, but if they see a white guy they're going to assume we're spies or special forces. That burns our mission, and I can't have that. Besides, do you know how to drive a boat?"

"No."

"Exactly."

"Don't blame me for that, Jais. You're the one who picked me over the other guys that tried out."

"I told you not to bring that up."

"You just...you said some weird shit to me during our interview."

"That's enough, David." His face turned to granite.

Unwilling to raise his suspicion any further, I fell silent.

Jais continued driving, and as the trees cleared the Jubba River appeared before us, its rippling waters extending five hundred feet to a far bank dotted with palm trees. Jais followed the trail as it turned left and paralleled the river, and then stopped the pickup as soon as the primitive village buildings were visible through the windshield. He put the transmission in neutral and cranked the parking brake, leaving the hotwired engine running as we exited the Hilux to warm air thick with the smell of seawater.

Jais reached into his combat pack in the bed to retrieve the boxy Iridium satellite phone and powered it on. He extended the antenna and dialed a programmed number, holding the phone to his ear. Adjusting my grip on the rifle, I turned my gaze east toward the ocean.

While Kismayo may have been reminiscent of a hundred other desert shitholes I had seen, Goobweyn was staggeringly beautiful.

The rising sun cast waves of shimmering sparkles across the river's graceful curves, culminating in a golden haze where it met the Indian Ocean. Clusters of palm trees leaned perilously over the water's edge, their fronds drifting with a warm morning breeze. The sky after the storm was a crystal, cloudless eternity rising over the earth and water, endlessly clear without a trace of precipitation.

Jais began speaking into the phone. "This is Bobcat Actual. Be advised, aircraft detour due to storm necessitated emergency bailout. Current location: vicinity of Goobweyn. Transitioning to boat for movement north on Jubba River, will establish hold-up site south of Jilib and report location prior to nightfall. Request reception party pick us up there—"

There was a long pause before he spoke again.

"Copy all. Continuing mission, will update when able. Out."

Collapsing the antenna, he turned off the phone and replaced it in his pack.

I said, "I didn't like that long pause in the middle of your conversation."

"The reception party is honoring the terms of the original agreement: pick up at the landing zone, not fifty miles away. They said the enemy presence is too strong along the river for them to come near it."

"Maybe our bosses need to be more persuasive."

"Don't I know it. Get used to this, David. The Outfit is at the bottom of a very long and mysterious food chain. Now wait here and try not to look so white."

Without another word he began walking along the shore into the village, carrying his rifle pointed barrel-down at his side.

The heat was going to be a beast to contend with, I thought as he walked away. While we weren't standing precisely on the equator, our mission had taken us just three degrees of latitude south of it. The sun's first rays beamed through me as if it were already midday, its stifling heat aided by the rag encompassing my head.

Looking back to the north, I saw Jais's hand raise in a friendly greeting as distant villagers clustered on the bank to receive him. I turned in a slow circle, my thoughts now shifting to more strategic matters.

Even in our present situation, stranded a prodigious distance from our intended destination, I was haunted by the chain of thought that had begun back in Kismayo, which now seemed a world away amid the sunrise. As had so often happened since Ian recovered me from the Dominican, I began considering the identity of a possible traitor. I had weighed the likelihood of Boss, Matz, and Ophie ad nauseam—but was now plagued by the notion that someone else had been lurking in the shadows, unnoticed.

Who could I have been missing? Who else could have known what was said during a meeting that had occurred months earlier with only my teammates in attendance?

The only answer, I realized with a gnawing sense of discomfort, was Ian.

He wasn't present that morning, but he was the only other person with access to the house and the ability to come and go freely. In that moment, it dawned on me that the Indian wasn't my sole source of intelligence.

Ian was.

He had provided all the information we had about the Handler and the organizations at war. After the team was killed, Ian had controlled everything I knew of the universe outside my compound in the Dominican, had supplied the notion of the survivor, and, for all I knew, had told the Indian exactly what information to feed me.

Could Ian work for the Handler?

My mind lurched through a stomach-churning sequence of events. Boss had told me that Ian led a team of guys who worked around the clock to obtain intelligence for us, and yet we never saw any of them. The only direct contact with the Handler I'd ever witnessed was Boss answering his phone to receive the final assignment to kill the Five Heads. When Boss had ended that call, he'd said, *And that was the Handler himself, not his assistant.* Ian was the only one not present for that conversation, and yet he had conveniently appeared the next day with all the information we needed to march to our deaths.

The buzz-saw rhythm of a boat motor approaching from the north cut through the sound of the idling truck engine, and I looked to its source.

The craft slicing through the water toward me was a small, white and blue boat perhaps twenty feet in length. Jais stood alone at the helm, rotating the steering wheel with one hand and pulling back on the throttle with the other.

I slung my rifle and carried both combat packs down to the bank, then set them on the sand and returned to the Hilux to remove the kit bags filled with our parachute equipment and cold weather gear. After performing a final check of the cab and bed to ensure we hadn't left anything behind, I hoisted the kit bags and shuffled toward the combat packs. By then, Jais had slowed the boat and was turning sharply toward me as the hull slid to a stop against the sand at the water's edge.

I saw six molded plastic seats and two yellow fuel cans on the floor of the boat.

"Nice score," I said, loading our combat packs and kit bags.

"Yeah," Jais said. "They can buy three more of these fine vessels for what I paid for this one, so everyone came away happy."

Pushing the hull with both arms, I took three wet steps through tepid water before leaping onto the bow and settling into a seat in front of the helm as the boat rocked. As we drifted backward, Jais increased the throttle and then turned a wide arc back the way he had come, hugging the east bank as we soared northward.

To our left, slim women in burkas carried yellow jugs toward the water's edge and a cluster of children waved to us with unintelligible shrieks. As we cruised past them, I saw a herd of a dozen or so lanky camels being driven to the water by boys with sticks and a pair of mules wandering along the bank, unsupervised. All of this whipped by in a blur before sandy shores and palm trees stretched ahead of us as the ground on either side of the river extended flat in both directions.

I pulled the *shemagh* down from my mouth, still considering whether Ian was under the Handler's employ. Above the metallic whine of the motor and the wind in our faces, I called, "My first African wildlife. Not exactly a safari."

Managing the wheel from his standing vantage point, Jais replied, "When your ass is running from a lion, you'll miss the camels. You okay? You look like you're getting seasick already."

I brushed the thought of Ian from my mind. "I'm fine. Mind if I lighten the load?"

"Go ahead."

Grabbing one of the kit bags, I heaved it over the side of the boat. The second followed suit, splashing into the surface of the Jubba and quickly sinking out of sight. I watched the trail of our wake curving with the shape of the river, my final glimpse of ocean replaced by an arid, desolate landscape that was soon devoid of any signs of life.

7

"Put your *shemagh* on!"

Jais's voice was sharp but as quiet as he could manage over the low, grumbling sound of the boat engine.

Wondering what he had spotted, I ducked my head, pulled the cloth over my face, and quickly tied it in place against the wind. Whatever havoc the tumultuous political situation had wrought in Somalia, the river remained tranquil—so far, the only signs of human life were a few decrepit fishing vessels.

In fact, the three hours we'd spent on the open water had almost been relaxing. Trees and foliage along the water provided shade from the sun's wrath, and the speed of the boat created a warm wind that cooled our sweaty faces. We had just one hour to go before we would pull our vessel into the forest and wait for nightfall. Then, we would proceed under the first bridge at Jilib, fully expecting to reach Dujuma and steal another vehicle by daybreak before continuing toward the landing zone.

After securing my *shemagh*, I looked up to see that, by scarcely ten in the morning on our first day in Somalia, we had been compromised.

Squinting through the dense mass of jade trees to our left, I caught intermittent glimpses of a filthy white van riding low on overburdened tires. The roof was loaded with four-foot bundles of cloth, and on top of that yellow barrels were strapped with single strands of rope. Two Somali men were perched like songbirds atop one of the bundles, peering toward us with their sandaled feet resting on the windshield.

Jais casually held up one hand, and one of the men waved back as the van rumbled southward on the west bank and disappeared from view behind the trees.

I said, "Where the fuck did that come from? We haven't even made it to Kamsuuma yet."

Jais accelerated the boat to full throttle, and the pitch of the engine went from a steady, dull roar to a high-pitched whine. "No idea," he called over the sound. "That road's not on our maps."

My pulse began racing as our boat carved a semicircle left along a bend in the river. Within seconds, we caught sight of a bridge—another key feature that our maps didn't depict. By the time we saw it, Jais could do nothing but maintain full throttle. I readied the Galil in my lap as we scanned the bridge before us.

It was a perfectly straight expanse of wooden X-frame rails suspended twenty feet over the muddy river. At its center stood a single militiaman.

He was dressed in a brown T-shirt under an olive chest rig like ours. His uncovered head was silhouetted against the sky alongside a sharp triangular shape that he held over his shoulder, pointed upward.

"RPG," I said, recognizing it as the cone of a rocket-propelled grenade.

Jais raised a fist and shouted, "Allahu Akbar!"

By way of response, the man on the bridge lowered the rocket launcher over his shoulder and aimed the cone toward us.

Jais kept the boat moving at full speed, and his next words were spoken with all the understatement of delivering a weather report.

"Take him, David."

By the time my name had left Jais's mouth, the rifle's buttstock was pressed firmly against my shoulder and the barrel was leveled with the man on the bridge. As I clicked the selector lever from safe to fire, I centered my crosshairs just above the man's chest rig, where I could now see a fixed-blade knife tied horizontally above his magazines.

I fired two rounds, the buttstock thumping into my shoulder with each shot, and the last thing I saw was a slight flutter in his T-shirt, as if a breeze had ruffled the fabric, before he dropped out of sight.

And that's how it worked most of the time in combat, I thought, even as I waited for him to emerge again with the rocket—there was no stuntman fall from the bridge with limbs flailing. They just...dropped out of sight.

My optic went dark as we cruised under the bridge, and I lowered my rifle to see Jais swerving the boat around the next curve in the river, where a dense blanket of forest guarded the banks on both sides.

For a split second, my mind didn't connect the flickering muzzle flare on the far side of the river with the audio of erupting machinegun fire; instead, I initially registered them as separate events in no way connected with the string of geysers that danced across the water in succession as they stitched their way toward our boat.

The first rocket launched from the far shore, a wispy streak of smoke marking its progress from the firing point to its impact on the near bank in front of our boat. It exploded in a cloud of flame and dirt that turned my head into a bell tower of painful ringing.

I raised my rifle and began returning fire—for lack of options more than anything else. My rounds were no match for a medium machinegun and an RPG firing from positions of cover and concealment, and when the second machinegun opened fire at us from farther up the river, I knew at once that they had us dead to rights.

Jais made a valiant effort to speed our boat through the kill zone until the second machinegun opened up. Moving forward or to the left would have led us into the spray of bullets, so he swerved right instead. I only became aware of this when the view through my optic suddenly shifted from the clear, distant view of bushes on the far shore to an unfocused blur of green immediately in front of me.

The boat ran into the bank at full speed, throwing me on top of our combat packs as we came to a stop with the engine still churning.

Jais may have yelled something to me, but my ears were still ringing from the RPG blast. All I cared about was getting our equipment and ourselves deep into the jungle as fast as possible, and so I picked up my combat pack and threw it off the boat.

The pack soared an outlandish distance into the brush—with a greater velocity than I ever could have dreamed of hurling it under normal circumstances—which was my first indication that adrenaline had seized control of my body. I grabbed Jais's combat pack and easily repeated the performance, watching it fly twenty feet into a grove of bushes.

As I snatched my rifle, Jais's hands were upon me, shoving me forward. I flew off the bow and rolled into a blanket of spiky grass, sensing his body landing beside me as successive bursts of machinegun fire began impacting the area around our abandoned boat.

We plunged violently forward through the brush, the thorns and sharp leaves slicing through our clothes and skin going virtually unnoticed as we ran deeper into the foliage, finding one combat pack and then another and donning them immediately. I reloaded my second magazine of mixed hollow points and armor-piercing rounds and looked over to see Jais scanning the vegetation to our front.

"Well," I said, pulling the *shemagh* down from my mouth, "at least we're on the right side of the river now."

"Baby steps, Rivers. You all right?"

"I'm going to miss being river pirates. You?"

"Don't get me started." He panted two quick breaths, a blanket of sweat appearing on his forehead. "There's no place for us to go, and they know it. They're going to come at us from the east. When they do, we need to hit them hard before they realize what's happening."

If the conversation had been occurring from a position of relative safety, I would have laughed in his face. Instead, I replied, "That shouldn't take long, because all we've got are two rifles and some goddamn American fighting spirit."

"All the more reason to make every round count. Come on."

He pushed himself to his feet. I followed suit, and together we plunged deeper into the forest.

* * *

The jungle we moved through wasn't a dripping rainforest teeming with life but rather a dense conglomeration of the same scrub brush and trees I would expect to see on a savannah. According to the map, our protection from outside view was comprised of a square kilometer at best; we were bordered on all sides by the river, open fields, or the main road along the western end of the city toward which we now ran.

A forest of that size didn't provide much in the way of hiding for two men known to enemy forces, and less so if the enemy in question had no incentive not to flush their quarry by wildly firing into the trees with crew-served weapons. We could still hear machinegun chatter from the far shore, and with the city of Kamsuuma just across the road at the forest's eastern edge, the militia on our side of the river would converge on us within minutes.

We raced eastward, trying to find the sole trail leading out of the forest into Kamsuuma proper. Before we could locate it, we heard a monstrously loud burst of heavy weapon fire.

Jais stopped suddenly and whispered, "There's our lifeline—that's a Dushka firing."

Through heaving breaths of hot jungle air, I replied, "So they've got a machinegun big enough to shoot down a helicopter. Explain to me how this helps our cause."

"It's too big to carry, which means it's on the back of a truck. And that truck is our only ride out of here unless we fuck it up. Now let's go find it."

Another burst of Dushka fire sounded to our front, this time followed by the supersonic crack of its rounds smashing through the trees. We continued moving and found the trail in short order, seeing that it was merely a set of tire tracks weaving among the dense vegetation that entombed us from outside view.

We had hoped to locate a sharp bend where we could set up a hasty L-shaped ambush. Instead, we stopped beside a slight turn in the otherwise straight path.

Jais said, "This is as good as we're going to get. I'm going to set up here to hit the driver head-on. I want you to move twenty meters up, find a position on the left, and take out the gunner from the side as soon as I open fire. Then we're riding that bitch out of here."

I shot off into the brush beside the trail, hearing a third burst of Dushka fire as I settled into position behind the biggest tree trunk I could find, located a scant fifteen feet off the tracks. If I moved any farther into the brush, I'd lose my view of the enemy truck when it approached.

For a few long moments, I heard no bird or insect calls, just my breath and the rustle of wind through the treetops. Soon, I detected the sound of the truck engine approaching.

The next burst of Dushka fire thundered through the forest, and a glimmer of flame became visible through the leaves as the gunner sprayed the bushes to my left in an attempt to draw us out of hiding. Branches and leaves rained to the forest floor amid cloudy streaks of incinerated bark that faded as quickly as they appeared. As the echo of the shots receded, I could hear the vehicle's engine once more.

As the first glimpse of the truck's bumper slid into view, the resolute focus of inevitability befell me. I wrapped my left hand around the tree trunk, thumb pointed out, and rested my rifle's handguard in the notch of my palm.

Rotating slightly, I angled my head toward a tan Hilux pickup visible under the swinging shape of an outlandishly long Dushka barrel that was being maneuvered by a standing gunner in a black *shemagh*. The Dushka's barrel was as long as the hood of the truck, though that was still less concerning than what I saw in the bed.

Enemy fighters were packed in the back, sitting atop some unseen surface with their legs hanging over the side of the truck, looking out. Five of them faced me, the barrels of their assault rifles and machineguns bobbing like medieval lances as the truck rumbled toward Jais. There must have been an equal number of men facing out the opposite side.

We were hopelessly outnumbered, and in the final moment before I opened fire, I recalled the last time I felt so frightened—in the woods outside the target house that Matz and I were about to enter, where I tried to conceal my shaking hands as he spoke.

"Don't worry about how many guys they have. What did I tell you before we left?"

"That we're only outgunned as long as we're missing."

"God, I love my job. Now go."

A cluster of white puffs burst out of the windshield—Jais was shooting the driver. I leveled my optic on the Dushka gunner and saw his standing profile vanish as I hammered two rounds just below his neck.

The truck wasn't quite broadside to me as I shifted my attention to the men in the back, firing a shot into each torso from right to left as fast as my aim would allow. I hit the man closest to the bumper before working my way back toward the cab, allotting two shots for each figure I saw along the way.

Just before the clatter of return fire, I heard a great wail of agony and pain as bodies spilled forward onto the ground and backward into the bed. By the time the truck rolled broadside to me, I had emptied my magazine and was ducking behind the tree to reload. Angling back around the tree to find the truck slowing to a halt, I began firing on the shapeless masses crumpled above the seating area in the bed. Between muzzle flashes, I caught a blur of movement. Jais was racing toward the truck, sprinting down the overgrown trail with his combat pack and rifle faster than I could have run on a track.

He fired a chaotic spread of shots as he moved, lacing bodies I couldn't see on the far side of the vehicle. Upon reaching the driver's door, he wrenched it open, flung a body out of the cab, and tossed in his rifle and combat pack before leaping inside and reversing toward me.

I ran forward to meet him, angling my barrel left and firing rounds into a row of bodies scattered along the trail. They were dressed in camouflage fatigues, some heads were wrapped in *shemaghs* and some not, and a few were trying to crawl until my optic crossed over their forms and I gunned them down for good.

Jais slammed on the brakes beside me. I scrambled atop a rear tire and into the bed, barely clearing the edge before he reversed down the trail and toward Kamsuuma.

I fell onto my side, finding the uneven surface below me to be a bloodied mass of bodies.

There were four men in the back with me, their figures prostrate on top of metal ammunition cans and wooden crates arranged around the bed as a seating platform. I struggled to sit upright, feverishly trying to assess whether any of them were a threat. I wanted to shoot them all by firing downward but couldn't risk severing a hydraulic line on the vehicle.

Regardless, I had zero chance of standing unassisted in the jarring truck bed as Jais floored it in reverse while trying not to hit the trees on either side of the narrow path. One thickly muscled arm rested on the doorframe as he leaned out the window to look behind him.

My vision was drawn to a glowing disc of light beyond the tailgate that grew larger as we glided toward it at the highest possible speed. As we approached, I realized with equal parts relief and dread that I was looking at the trailhead at the end of the forest, beyond which lay only open terrain and sky.

"Ten seconds!" I yelled to Jais. I dumped my combat pack and pulled myself up a metal tripod crudely welded to the bottom of the bed, atop which the Dushka was bobbing from a single pintle mount. Grasping one of the vertical handles with my left hand, I found the parallel handle and hoisted myself to my feet, spinning the heavy mass of metal around until the business end was oriented toward the exposed ground outside the forest.

I lined up the giant stud of the front sight post with the trailhead, having only moments to check that the belt of ammunition still ran under the gun's feed tray cover. The pointed tips of the six-inch bullets clanged into the metal walls of the long ammo can extending to my left, and I glanced around the weapon for a safety lever before we burst out of the trees into the blinding sunlight.

Jais careened into a wide turn that swung our back end onto the main road leading to the bridge, where two trucks identical to our own now sped toward us between the X-frame cross braces. The lead truck's driver and gunner clearly saw me. In the time it took me to align my front sight post with their windshield, it occurred to me that, in my *shemagh* and from four hundred feet away, they hadn't yet realized that I wasn't one of their comrades. In a flash of mild panic, I wondered whether my new gun's safety lever was activated or not and pulled the dual trigger with both index fingers.

The weapon roared to life with a pulsing cadence of explosions that jarred my ribcage.

I squinted through the rear ladder sight with both arms fully flexed to maintain my point of aim on the lead truck, which erupted in streaming clouds of smoke before a plume of flame shot skyward. Jais put our vehicle into drive and accelerated forward. The truck I'd been shooting was now stationary, completely ablaze, and blocking my view of the trail vehicle. I unleashed another long burst of gunfire. When I finally released the triggers, I heard Jais yelling, "GUN FRONT!"

Traversing the giant weapon required me to circle around the tripod mount and step on the bodies of militia fighters. I swung the barrel left to see the village of Kamsuuma sweeping by in a blur of tightly packed mud and tin buildings. Gunshots erupted from our front a fleeting moment before I located their source.

A hundred meters away were dozens of armed men in fatigues and black *shemaghs*, a line of black flags falling as they scrambled to either side of the road and out of the way of our truck. Muzzle flashes sparkled among their ranks, the cracks of incoming bullets soon buried beneath the thundering boom of my Dushka as I swept the rocking muzzle to rake a storm cloud of dirt and human flesh from one side of the street to the other.

I released the trigger as we closed upon them, spinning the barrel behind me as our tires thumped over bodies in the street, nearly knocking me down in the process. Once I saw the green shapes of uniformed bodies off the driver side, I continued firing as I completed a full 360 with the gun.

Without time to judge if any of them were still alive, I simply didn't want to stop shooting the Dushka—its recoil was unlike anything I'd experienced, and the ability to project force after we'd turned the odds in a few minutes of intense fighting felt addictive.

Jais shouted, "Cease fire, goddammit! We're going to need that ammo."

I saw the dispersed formation of fallen men receding into the distance and swung the barrel forward. The buildings of Kamsuuma gave way to endless rectangular plots of low-lying green crops as we sped northeast on the main road.

Bending my knees, I looked through the blood-stained rear windshield to see bullet holes on either side of my legs. The front windshield seemed to have taken an even greater number. "You shot or what?" I asked.

"Took some glass shrapnel, but I'll live. You did pretty good with that Dushka."

"I don't know where this thing has been all my life."

"First time shooting one?"

"Yeah, and judging by the way this mission is going so far, it won't be my last. I'm going off the gun to search these bodies; holler at me if you see anything up front."

I knelt beside the dead militiamen, used a knife to cut their chest rigs free, and patted down their pockets before tossing their bodies over the tailgate. Then I did a quick inventory of the crates in the back.

"We've got six grenades, three AKs, eleven magazines, and around twenty rounds for the Dushka," I called to Jais. "And there are two full fuel cans back here."

"Be glad there are fuel cans, because we've only got a quarter of a tank."

"For once, why couldn't we have stolen a vehicle that's actually been filled up?"

"Doesn't matter. We've only got forty miles to cover before we can go off road and head north toward the landing zone, and with the cans in the back we're good to hook."

"Until they come looking for us."

"That's what I meant. Get the weapons and ammo sorted, David. We might have a hell of a fight ahead."

8

After checking that there were no vehicles within view, I knelt to my combat pack and sipped from a flexible hose to gain a mouthful of hot river water tinted with the medicinal taste of plastic and iodine tablets.

It was almost noon, the heat soaring into the mid-nineties as we rolled down the red dirt path extending as far as I could see in either direction.

We had passed little in the way of traffic aside from the occasional van or motorcycle overburdened with people and cargo, the occupants acting remarkably unperturbed by the sight of our bullet-ridden pickup mounted with a heavy machinegun.

I had kept my *shemagh* and sunglasses on and my sleeves rolled down over shooting gloves that now served a purpose beyond hiding my skin color. Other than its wood handles, my Dushka had become too hot to touch.

Since leaving Kamsuuma, it had taken us a full two and a half hours to cover forty-five miles. Our movement was slowed by a twelve-mile stretch of alternating dirt trails and off-road movement as we detoured around the town of Jilib, where militia checkpoints would surely have been bolstered in search of the captured truck headed their way. Now we were on a different road headed east, making good time as we watched for a break in the dry riverbed that was thinning enough to soon be passable by truck.

Once we crossed it, we had a scant thirty miles of off-road driving to reach our landing zone.

From behind the wheel, Jais called, "You see a break in that riverbed yet?"

"Not yet, but we should be able to cross it soon. Shame it didn't rain this far north, because I'm running out of water fast."

"Then drink less," he yelled.

"Easy for you to judge from inside the truck. It feels like the surface of the sun back here."

"It's almost noon on the equator. Were you expecting Greenland?"

"Don't give me that. We would have been there by now if you hadn't taken so long on the Jilib bypass."

"If we hadn't found a cross-country route around Jilib, this truck would be a pile of twisted metal right now. Besides, I offered to switch you out on the gun and you refused."

"I'm trying to pull my weight on this op, okay?"

"Don't act like you're back there for my benefit. Since you shot the Dushka, it's become the other woman in our relationship."

"You're wrong about that, Jais. Since I shot the Dushka, *you've* become the other woman."

I scanned the riverbed to my left as the crease in the land continued to narrow. We'd be moving off road again within minutes, and once we'd crossed into the open desert and began driving northward, our odds of being effectively pursued by the enemy would lessen by the minute. We were virtually guaranteed to make our landing zone; then, the only question became whether the Silver Widow's reception party would still be there to greet us twelve hours past our anticipated parachute landing. If they weren't, I felt certain that Jais would be able to use the satellite phone to arrange either our linkup or extraction.

Either way, we had overcome tremendous odds and reacted seamlessly to a tumultuous situation. It was a solid beginning to my reputation in the Handler's private army, one that would be further bolstered if we were able to bring the case back home. And with Jais ascending the ranks of the organization beyond the fenced perimeter of the Complex, our smooth working relationship was likely to benefit me in the future, one way or another. I should have been ecstatic.

Instead, I found my thoughts drifting back to Ian.

My heart sank as I considered the facts. His participation in the final mission—and its fallout—seemed the most damning evidence in favor of him working for the Handler all along. Only Ian knew my exact location at the mortar firing point, but a seemingly random patrol had somehow walked straight into me. I'd barely escaped alive before reaching a car with him behind the wheel.

And while he had been driving when Karma was killed in an ostensibly sporadic burst of gunfire, Ian and I had somehow emerged unharmed. But why wouldn't he have shot me to achieve total closure?

There was an explanation for that, too, I thought grimly. All the old hands who knew too much about the Handler's operation were conveniently killed on their way back from an ambush point whose location, again, only Ian knew. By letting me survive, Ian had just gained a naïve, newly-trained team member with unlimited motivation to kill.

Moreover, Ian had been the only one to enter the garage of the target house, where he'd supposedly acquired the existing assassination plot from the Five Heads—and he had admitted to not sharing that information with Boss. Even my unquestioning belief in the so-called attempt to kill the Handler while I was in the Dominican Republic represented a blind leap of faith. Ian had subsequently refused to show me the footage of the supposed failed assassination attempt. Considered objectively, Ian's many ominous warnings about the Handler could very well have been mere ruses to direct my wrath toward an unseen entity, thereby absolving Ian himself from suspicion.

If Ian did work for the Handler, it would explain nearly every mystery since the team's path had crossed mine on the night I killed Peter.

Jais called, "Why are you so quiet back there?"

"Enjoying the scenery," I said, snapping back to the present moment. "We're actually going to pull this thing off, aren't we?"

"You've got me in charge. Was there ever any doubt?"

I nodded vigorously. "When we landed a hundred miles from our destination last night, I'd say yes, there was plenty of doubt. Roughly speaking, I thought our life expectancies had dropped to about one hour. I thought you were crazy for not calling the helicopter."

"That's the genius of the Outfit. The cost of failure is worse than anything the enemy could do, and that inspires a degree of commitment you wouldn't get any other way."

"I'd say the militias here in Somalia are a pretty powerful motivator as well."

"Lesser of two evils. The Outfit is worse."

"Then why are you working for it?"

He paused. "The more missions you run out of the Complex, David, the more you'll see that the Handler is the greatest force for good you'll ever serve."

I smiled to myself, remembering Ian heralding the exact opposite while briefing Boss's team. "We just smoked about two dozen fighters in probably the wildest upset in Somali sports history because it was safer than calling our own bosses after God tried to kill us in the sky last night. 'Force for good' isn't the term that springs to mind."

"You're assuming it's not for a higher purpose."

"I'm not assuming. But this case better be worth it."

He didn't respond immediately, leaving me to wipe the stinging sweat out of my eyes as I scanned the road around us. After two and a half hours of standing, every joint ached.

"The case isn't as important as what he's going to do with it," Jais said after a few more moments of silence. "If you saw the bigger picture, you'd know that his refusal to accept failure—on this mission more than most—is a mark of true character."

"I'm not doubting you, brother, but let's not pretend either of us ended up here to pursue philanthropy."

"'Course not. Until I made it into the Outfit, the only thing I cared about was money."

"You don't strike me as greedy."

"I'm not, but that all changed when it came to my momma."

"You're serious?"

"Hundred percent. I don't know if you had both parents growing up, but I just had my mom."

"Tell me about her."

"She was everything to me, David. Did I tell you I was almost a minor league baseball player?"

"Definitely not."

"No shit. Didn't even make the high school tryouts freshman or sophomore year, and she made me train so hard I had farm team scouts coming to my senior games..."

I squinted ahead to a shallow dip in the terrain marred by previous vehicle tracks and called, "Break in the riverbed, fifty feet up."

"All right, I see it. Let's get this truck off the road. Thirty miles to the landing zone and we're home free. One way or the other."

As he steered off the road and onto the bumpy dirt descending toward the riverbed, I saw sunlight glinting off a windshield on the road far to our front.

I called out, "Vehicle front."

"If they follow us off road, you better make them regret it."

He steered along the winding trail as it descended sharply into the riverbed. Slowing to a near stop, he nosed the pickup downward and then accelerated to gain enough momentum to make it up the far side. The other vehicle continued approaching, though I was still unable to distinguish what type it was.

I called out, "Jais, let's find a spot to watch the riverbed. If that vehicle follows us, I want to hit them while they're at that chokepoint."

He continued driving, cutting a hard right between a cluster of low trees that concealed the riverbed. I talked him forward until a small break in the vegetation revealed the crossing point.

"Three more feet...two...stop."

I oriented the Dushka on our own tracks where they traversed the riverbed, now barely visible beside the main road. The trees to our front obscured my visibility, but I knew we were well-concealed. An onlooker would have to look at us directly from the low ground to make out my weapon through the leaves, and by then it would be too late.

It wasn't until the approaching vehicle slowed to turn off the road that I could make it out—the Hilux pickup was almost a mirror image of ours. A militiaman swept his machinegun barrel over the ground to his front as the truck slowed to descend into the riverbed.

I waited for the vehicle to commit to the off-road turn and roll into the low ground, its momentum slowing to a near-halt where the terrain rolled upward. Then I pulled the dual triggers of my machinegun, holding the front sight post steady as the Hilux nearly disappeared in a sudden cloud of smoke and sand. The gunner bowled over and the vehicle came to a complete stop. I released another burst to ensure the engine was disabled; the back blast from my muzzle poured a flash of scalding air at my face with every massive round I fired.

I saw flames emerge under their hood and fired my last bullet through the Dushka.

"Got him," I called to Jais. "Drive."

As he began pulling forward, I caught sight of a second pickup screeching to a halt on the main road, this time with a gunner who leveled his PKM machinegun in our general direction. He unleashed a burst that decimated the treetops behind us.

I dropped to the bed as Jais floored the gas, wheeling our truck through a labyrinth of brush and trees sprawled across the ground.

Jais yelled, "It doesn't sound like you got him."

I pulled myself back up behind the gun, hearing successive machinegun blasts to our rear as the remaining gunner probed for our position.

I hesitated. "It's a second truck."

"All right, let's find a good hiding spot and run the same play."

"We're, ah...we're out of ammo for the big gun."

"Is that a fact?"

"Yeah. I suppose you can thank the militia assholes for shooting so much of it at us in the forest."

"Don't blame the militia assholes for your inability to conserve ammo, David."

I puffed a breath and shouted, "It was my first time shooting a Dushka —I can't be held accountable for my actions. But I can fix this."

"Enlighten me."

"I've got grenades."

He laughed. "Been a while since I played baseball, but I'm pretty confident their machinegun can outrange my grenade throw by a kilometer or so. Much less yours."

"Yeah, yeah, I get that. So I'll jump off, hide next to our tracks, and roll a grenade under their truck when it passes."

"Unless it blows under a fuel line you're just going to end up with a lot of pissed-off survivors in a truck that won't move."

"So come back for me fast once you hear the explosion. Come on, you keep trying to get me to make decisions. Can you think of anything better?"

"No. That still doesn't make your idea a good one."

The low-lying trees and scrub brush clinging to the rugged terrain required a series of chance detours. Jais's fleeting choices of right versus left could spell the difference between a continued journey and a dead end, so I had to move quickly. Finding concealment for my one-man ambush wouldn't be difficult, particularly from the eyes of a driver and a gunner trying to catch glimpses of our tire tracks where the hard-packed ground gave way to sandy patches that betrayed our passage.

But I had a harder time locating terrain that would provide physical cover from a close-range grenade explosion.

I spotted a washout to our right side, where the ground dropped steeply to a depth of two or three feet. The elevation difference was packed with dry scrub brush that filled the void. It probably wasn't enough to protect me from a grenade blast, I thought briefly, but the rippling crack of machinegun rounds soaring through the sky caused me to reevaluate my risk tolerance.

"Slow down," I said, picking up my Galil and feeling the truck decelerate as we approached the washout. "I'm off to save your life, buddy."

The last words I heard from Jais were as nonchalant as almost everything else he spoke.

"Don't let the tailgate hit you on your way out."

I leapt off the right side of the truck, keeping my legs together and knees slightly bent as if taking a hard parachute landing.

It was a well-measured precaution, because a second later I smashed through a dry bush that crumbled on impact, its thorns punching into my right side as I slammed against the hard dirt. My roll down the washout was arrested by the tangled mass of branches and thorns that gradually held me in place like Velcro, and I hissed with pain as I pushed myself upright.

Then I scrambled left along the trail, throwing myself down again beside a shoulder-height plant representing my best odds of concealment from the oncoming Hilux. I pushed my way through the brush, African dust coating my teeth, and positioned my head beside the two-and-a-half-foot dirt ledge rising toward Jais's tire tracks. Setting my rifle down to my right, I rolled onto my side and fumbled a grenade out of the side pouch of my chest rig as I heard the enemy truck's approach.

I pulled the safety pin on the grenade, keeping the lever compressed to its metal body. Lifting my head slightly toward the blazing, cloudless sky, I tried to gauge the distance of the truck's engine above the omnipresent high-pitched ringing in my ears. Before long, I could hear the passengers conversing urgently in a foreign language.

Opening my hand to allow the curved lever to spring free from the grenade body, I counted down the five-second fuse as if it were a BASE jump.

One thousand, two thousand...

I pushed myself up on one hand and gently rolled the grenade between Jais's tire tracks as the enemy truck closed in on my left.

A man onboard the truck yelled something as I collapsed back down, feeling the shards of brittle thorns in my skin as I flattened myself into the earth. An AK-47 opened fire just over my head as I plugged both ears with my fingers, mouth ajar in anticipation of the grenade's overpressure. I tensed my body and waited for a bullet to hit me, hoping for a grazing wound at worst.

The AK clacked off four rounds on full automatic before my body was jolted by the grenade's detonation. The alarming blast was stifled under an even greater explosion as a scalding shockwave flashed across my body.

I opened my eyes with the certainty that my clothes were ablaze and instead saw a black sky. As I released my fingers from my ears, I could hear the moaning wail of disoriented survivors above the snapping groan of flames. I inhaled a cloud of smoke-filled dust and nearly retched.

Grabbing my rifle in one hand, I rose to a knee. As I cleared the berm amid the clanging in my head, I saw the hollow eyes of a Somali fighter of perhaps sixteen or seventeen years old looking at me from three feet away, his body prone on the ground.

There was no time to consider whether he was alive or armed as I pointed the Galil, its muzzle almost touching his forehead as I fired. Then I shifted my aim right, toward the truck that rolled to a stop five meters beyond the blast.

The grenade resulted in a great cloud of black smoke billowing from the engine and tires as orange flames licked the sides of the truck. Before I could shift my optic onto the truck bed, a pair of muzzle flashes pierced the smoke like stars in the darkness.

A spray of sand stung my eyes as bullets impacted the ridge I'd been aiming over, and I dropped back down as survivors in the bed fired automatic weapons. With my rifle cradled between bent elbows, I writhed in a crawling motion over sharp plants and jagged rocks, clumsily following the washout as it descended away from the trail.

Blinking hard to clear my vision as I slithered belly-down over the sand, I saw the washout descending far enough below ground level for me to crouch there without being seen. I rose and ran, keeping my figure bent as I gained distance from the ambush position.

The gunshots had ceased, and I now heard two men shouting back and forth. I stopped, readied my rifle's buttstock into my shoulder, and stood to aim over the dirt mound before me.

I saw both men moving among the scattered brush to my front. The more distant of the two was whirling away from me with his AK-47, turning to face the sound of a redlining truck engine as Jais's pickup crested off the trail toward him. The closer man, holding a machinegun at his waist, did the same, sweeping his barrel toward the truck. I prioritized him through my sight and stitched three rounds between his shoulder blades.

He fell as I transitioned left, leveling my crosshairs on the last man standing as he emptied half a magazine before the truck's front bumper hit him head-on. His body careened sideways with a sudden momentum that sent his rifle bouncing my direction with a series of jarring metallic clangs.

The truck skidded to a halt, a soaring cloud of dust rising like a ghost that had left its body behind.

I jumped atop the berm and raised a hand toward Jais as he yelled, "I've got these two. Go search the bodies in the road!"

"Moving!" I yelled back, running up the washout toward the column of black smoke drifting slowly from the trail.

The barrel of an abandoned PKM pointed skyward, crowning the vehicle as a monument to death that would remain a fixed landmark in the Somali desert until the elements washed it away. I fired two rounds into the single motionless body in the trail before moving to the teenager I'd shot in the head.

A red splatter shot across the sand from his fractured skull as I kicked him onto his back. Any horror I may have felt at the sudden carnage was swept away by a tide of sheer relief at our own survival. I slung his AK-47 across my left shoulder and stripped three magazines from his chest rig, sliding them into a cargo pocket before taking a single plastic canteen from a pouch on his belt.

I jogged to the other body lying face-down on the trail, then roughly grabbed his sleeve and turned him over. His head rolled to face me and I jumped back, overcome by a chill of horror as my breathing was reduced to sharp, panicked gasps.

My world narrowed from the horizon-split sand and sky extending in all directions to invisible oceans until all was darkness but the man before me.

His face was half-covered with his *shemagh*. The flesh of his visible cheek was singed an alien crimson hue mottled by blackened flesh. A single exposed eye wept profusely amid the burns, the pupil almost iridescent beneath a torrent of tears.

I stared at him and he at me, the crackle of flames from the destroyed truck becoming increasingly distorted. My head grew dizzier as his visible eye flicked back and forth between mine.

I was jarred to reality when Jais shook my shoulder, his voice sounding as if I were hearing it underwater.

"David! David!"

I looked up.

Our truck was now facing north on the trail, idling in front of the enemy vehicle. Jais squinted into my eyes just as Ian had when he found me in the Dominican Republic, trying to see if I was drunk or not.

"David!" he yelled again.

I blurted, "I haven't gotten his ammo yet."

Jais looked terrified, the expression shattering his normal composure. "Forget the ammo. Our vehicle is fucked—a bullet grazed the radiator hose. It could burst any minute, and we still have thirty miles to go if they don't find us first. We need to get as far north as we can."

9

The truck's engine noise was suddenly muffled under a high-pitched hissing sound blasting from under the hood. Without warning, a rancid smell like burning chalk wafted into my face. I coughed as I stood behind the now-useless Dushka, my vantage point serving only to watch for signs of pursuit.

"What in the hell is that stench?" I yelled.

Jais braked amid a wide patch of flat earth flanked by distant plants, killing the engine once the truck came to a stop. The hissing subsided, leaving us to the desert silence.

"Boiling radiator fluid," Jais said eventually. "And that sound was it spraying under the hood. If we keep going, the engine will explode."

It had taken us over an hour to drive eighteen miles northward, during which I had seen no movement behind us—no dust clouds, people, or animals, just endless dirt and scrub brush under the hazy swelter of a relentless sun.

I parted chapped lips to croak, "Explain why that would matter at this point?"

He opened his door and stepped out, then reached back inside for his rifle before surveying the land around us. Only then did he look at me, his face holding an amused expression.

I knew what he was going to say before he opened his mouth.

"You tell me, David."

I sighed. "Really, Jais? We have to do this now?"

"They'll be following our tracks, so make it quick."

"Because we want them to think we ran out of gas so they try to fill it up to get their mobile Dushka back and get incinerated by the booby traps we're about to set."

He nodded approvingly. "Old Faithful here just became the last thing standing between us and them, and I want it to explode if they look at it wrong. Unless you were looking forward to hauling the weight of all those grenades for the next"—he paused as he consulted the GPS on his wrist—"12.9 miles."

Instead of voicing my concern, I said, "Well, my bag's already a lot lighter now that it's not weighed down with...what's that word again? Oh yeah. Water."

It wouldn't be a great distance to cover under normal circumstances, but nothing about our circumstances qualified as normal. In truth, we faced a grave lack of water, temperatures in the nineties, and a solid twenty-four hours of being awake, much of which had been spent fighting for our lives.

Jais rifled through his pack, found the Iridium satellite phone, and turned it on. "We'd be riding that last enemy vehicle all the way to the landing zone if you didn't waste it with a grenade like a dick idiot."

Ignoring him, I tossed our combat packs sideways one at a time, their weight now a fraction of what we had jumped with since we were nearly out of water and had consumed a majority of our food rations. Then I handed him my rifle and gestured to the bed. "You told me to hit a fuel line, and I followed orders. I'll put a grenade under a fuel can back here."

Jais took it from me, the phone tucked between his ear and shoulder as he waited for the satellite connection. He leaned my rifle against my combat pack, then opened the fuel door and unscrewed the cap. "Put one with the machinegun, too. And toss one of the empty fuel cans down here."

I picked up a red, five-gallon jug and pitched it over the side for him to situate so it looked like it had been abandoned in despair. Then I reached into the wooden crate that held the captured grenades and plucked out a duo before lowering it to the ground for Jais. I knelt down in the bed, lining up the first grenade over the fuel tank and pulling one of the full fuel cans toward me.

"I'm ready to go live when you are, boss."

"Go ahead." Then Jais said into the phone, "This is Bobcat Actual. Current grid to follow..."

Taking a breath, I grasped a metal ring and delicately slid the pin out of the grenade, keeping the lever compressed with my other hand. Then I gently set it lever-down in the bed and laid the fuel can over it. Slowly spreading my fingers away from the grenade, I deftly withdrew my hand.

"...confirm all. Be advised, we escaped heavy contact and are currently under enemy pursuit. Critically low on food and water. Vehicle disabled, transitioning to foot movement due north toward landing zone. Request reception party move south to locate us..."

I rose very deliberately to a standing position and then lifted the Dushka handles enough to slip my second grenade between the body of the machinegun and its mount. After lowering the Dushka until its weight compressed the grenade lever, I inched out the pin and then pocketed it.

I rested a gloved hand fondly atop the feed tray cover and whispered, "Fare thee well, Dushka. You always deserved better than me."

"...continue until link-up complete or unable to proceed further. This is our final transmission."

I glanced over to see him turning off the phone, and then I crept to the tailgate as if walking on a bed of eggshells. Gingerly lowering myself to the ground, I stepped back from the truck with a long, self-indulgent exhale.

As Jais was packing away the phone in his combat pack, I asked, "Those assholes coming to get us or what?"

"Unconfirmed, but I was able to relay our position, so that's a start. Get ready to move. I'll booby-trap the cab and then we'll step off."

He approached the passenger door as I donned my combat pack, adjusted the shoulder straps, and hoisted my rifle to the ready. I walked a safe distance from the truck in case Jais had an accident while arranging his grenades.

I raised the optic to my eye and scanned the landscape to our south but saw no movement or rising dust to indicate immediate pursuit. Then I lowered my rifle and looked toward the horizon, which was flattened in a blur of rust-colored dirt and patches of plant life that became sparser as the land extended.

Jais joined me as I gazed off into the distance. "We're going to haul ass until we get about a mile from this deathtrap. Then we can slow down for the long haul."

I nodded and graciously bowed. "After you, my liege."

He began walking as briskly as one could manage without breaking into a run, and I struggled to keep up with his long, easy strides. By then, the sun was descending from its zenith to cast our shadows slightly to the right, where they crawled over the baked earth and dry plants as we proceeded north toward our landing zone.

* * *

Jais slowed his tremendous walking pace so suddenly that I almost ran into him from behind.

"All right," he said, "we've covered a mile. Let's keep it slow and steady for the next twelve."

"Good idea," I answered, moving alongside him. I kept just far enough to his right that the long Galil barrel wouldn't bump into him. "This would have been so much easier if we had just jumped on target."

"I would have settled for our truck making it all the way north," Jais said. "But look at the bright side—at least we didn't land in the ocean last night."

"Don't remind me. It's only been a couple months since my last drowning."

"Well, the test worked. Sergio chose a good crop to interview for this job."

"Did Sergio recruit you, too?"

"No, I had this hairy Iranian dude named Roshan—"

He stopped speaking, halting abruptly at the sight of a strange white framework rising to waist-height ahead of us. "What is that? A horse?"

We approached the immense, sun-bleached spinal cord arced over the dirt, suspended as if prostrate in prayer by a pelvic bone and shoulders that disappeared into the earth.

"Camel, maybe," I said over a blast of hot breeze rolling across us. "He was probably telling himself he had enough water to make the landing zone, too."

We walked around the skeleton. "What were we talking about?" he asked.

"The drowning event."

"Oh yeah. Anyway, it's a great test."

I released a quick laugh before I could stop myself. "Bullshit. I was hypothermic before I even went into the water. I'm surprised they could revive me."

He shook his head. "That's no accident. They make sure you're hypothermic, because the cold slows your vitals and forces your body to conserve oxygen. That's how they can do it without inducing brain damage. If they ran the same event in warmer temperatures, it would turn you into a vegetable or kill you."

I considered that for a moment.

As much as I'd been in a claustrophobic panic after being pulled from the water, not to mention the many nights since then that I'd burst awake in a gasping struggle to breathe, in hindsight I didn't recall the event with any particular feeling of dread. Instead, its memory was haloed by a resistant willingness akin to the initial plunge from the highest hill of a rollercoaster. For all my chronic and compulsive flirting with disaster, for all my hyper-sexual pull toward death, I had never crossed over as I had in that steel drum.

And in the wake of the rolling gunfights culminating in our lonely walk across the desert, I began to second-guess myself. Maybe I actually *did* want to run with the Outfit—not out of revenge, but out of a true calling. In a world defined by precious few moments where I felt truly alive, much less wanted to remain living, a job that tied my very existence to the evasion of death seemed as natural as drinking.

I asked, "Did you have to do the same test?"

"Everyone goes through one variant or another, but the location and scenario change over time. It's all designed to seem random, but it's not.

Even the way they bind your arms is a deliberate preparation for revival so candidates can't fight off the medical staff. It's all rehearsed."

"So what happens to the guys who confess instead of keeping their mouth shut about the task? How do they escape the scenario?"

"They don't. Everyone goes in the water. When someone confesses, they're just not resuscitated. Then it's off to the acid bath for the chemist on staff to supervise total decomposition. Last I heard, the average was around three lost for every new recruit. In some rounds, nobody makes it."

"That's crazy."

"Crazy?"

"Yes, Jais."

He shot me an unsympathetic glance. "That's called responsibility. The guys standing behind the mirror need to know that anyone they choose for the next job isn't going to quit on them. You get me?"

"Yeah, I guess."

"You recognized that guy coming off the plane at the Complex."

"He put out a few cigarettes on me. Hard to forget that face."

"You'd better start appreciating the genius of the selection process. Because once you get some seniority in the Outfit, you're going to be a part of running it."

I watched my boots drift for a few steps before asking, "Have you helped run it before?"

"A few times. Everyone has to before they get to lead a mission."

"How do you deal with that? I mean, I get killing in combat, but what about just dumping motherfuckers into a river?"

"Look at it this way: you're maintaining the sanctity of the Outfit and the organization it protects. It's about loyalty, David."

I opened and closed my mouth, feeling as if lockjaw was setting in as my dehydration worsened. "You know, you never finished your story about ending up in the Outfit. Before we found that break in the riverbed, you were about to be a major league baseball player."

"Ha. I wouldn't say that—minors, maybe. But Momma wouldn't have that. Wanted me to be the first in the family with a college degree."

"You get a scholarship?"

"Yeah, buddy. An ACL injury ended that real quick, though, and I had to start racking up debt to graduate."

"College loans," I said with a knowing nod. "Best military recruiting tool since the draft."

"Fuckin' A, man. Had to join for debt repayment, but I missed the fraternity of baseball and ended up finding it when I went over to special operations. Buddy of mine left the service and went to one of the para-military teams picking up jobs from the Outfit, and he wanted me to come over and work with him. Eventually, I did."

"Paramilitary team money was better than government pay?"

He gasped suddenly, and I turned just in time to see him fall, his left leg buckling before he smashed into the dirt, cursing.

I reached out to help him to his feet, and he reluctantly accepted my hand. I leaned back to hoist him up as he slowly rose to a standing position. Then he shook out his left leg, his face strained in anguish.

I asked, "ACL flaring up again?"

Jais continued walking without looking at me, then called over his shoulder, "Just shut the fuck up for a while, David."

Soon thereafter, he withdrew into an inner sanctum of pain, though whether physical or emotional I couldn't tell.

I said nothing, continuing alongside him in silence.

* * *

Our shadows lengthened considerably as the sun fell to our left, casting shallow rays that bathed the desert in a rose hue. Pant legs starched with dried sweat turned to sandpaper against my inner thighs, the chafing taking precedence over the throbbing objections of my knees.

Above all, the lust for water rose to unfathomable levels of desire.

I could see Jais favoring his right leg as we proceeded, his limp worsening with each quarter mile.

He stopped before another bleached skeleton.

"What's wrong?" I said.

He just nodded toward the ground.

I looked closer and saw the remains were human, half a ribcage curling above the dirt beside a skull lying on its side. The face glared hollowly with a sand-packed interior visible through every orifice, its remarkably white teeth biting onto sand with an open jaw.

We trudged on in silence. Less than a minute later, Jais suddenly fell sideways, landing on his side with a "Fuck!"

I sat on the ground beside him before he could object, facing the way we had come. Leaning on my combat pack, I aimed my rifle at the horizon and scanned for movement through my optic. "Nobody. Take five, man."

He grunted and sat up, and together we faced our own tracks receding into the distance.

We remained in place for a few minutes before he broke the silence. "Bad luck to stop next to human remains?"

"Groundless superstition." I pulled at the long hose clipped to my shoulder strap, indulging in a long mouthful of murky, iodine-cured river water until the liquid drained to nothing. I swallowed. "That's the last of my Jubba River refill."

"I ran out about a mile ago."

"Lucky thing we won't have sweat stinging our eyes much longer."

"Lesser men would call that a medical emergency."

I nodded. "Stalwart warriors always look for the bright side. At least we don't have wives to come home to."

"You're too young to get married anyway."

"My fiancée was sleeping with my best friend. That count?"

"Come talk to me when your wife leaves you for your stepbrother."

"You're kidding."

"I'm not."

"You kill him?"

"No. I wished them the best and left."

"Don't fuck with me."

"Have you ever let anybody down?"

Karma's head exploded in the seat beside me, the slap of her brain matter hot and stinging against my face. "Yes."

"Did you mean to deal them a crushing disappointment?"

Her body jumped in a gruesomely animated motion as the truck sped away. The acid rose in my throat. "No."

"If you could go back and change what you did, would you?"

"I'd give anything in the world."

Jais nodded, his point made. "We're all the same victim and the same perpetrator, David. Before any of us is guilty or persecuted, we are all human. The people who wronged us are having the same thoughts as the people we've wronged. So what's our responsibility to others? It's to accept their humanity, whether it benefited us or not."

I saw Karma again, this time in the glowing room of my dreams as she handed me the revolver. I said, "Maybe you just haven't failed anyone badly enough."

"I've done worse than you ever could."

"Try me."

"My old team used to do outsourced work, like I said. My ACL injury got worse—like it is now—and I finally had to get surgery. My team went on a mission while I was recovering, and they were all killed. The Outfit gave me a call to come try out after that."

"Goddamn, I'm—I'm sorry. I didn't know." But my sympathy soon faded behind a flash of anger.

The Indian was wrong.

The single source that Ian had blindly trusted, now in exile far outside the organization, was receiving reports so diluted by the time they reached him that they were now the copy of a copy, their edges blurred into obscurity. The Indian had prophesized a lone survivor that I would come face-to-face with. That much had come true, I realized—just not with someone from Boss's team. Nor was Jais a betrayer, but instead a regretful survivor haunted by the same lifelong curse of shame and remorse for living that I was.

Jais continued, "I keep it together most of the time. But not a day goes by that I don't wish I got killed with my team."

"It wasn't your fault," I said hollowly, speaking the words I knew I should.

"Survivor's guilt is a motherfucker, David. And there's no outliving that."

"What about everything you just said about empathy?"

"That's the part I struggle with. I can forgive my worst betrayers, but never myself."

I tried to swallow, feeling my parched throat contract. Then I stared at the bones amid the dirt before speaking again. "Last summer, after I got discharged from the Army and before I got the call to try out for the Outfit—"

A crashing noise tumbled thinly across the desert like the sound of faraway thunder.

We squinted toward a tiny plume of dark smoke in the distance rising upward like a lighthouse.

I said, "Guess they found our truck."

Jais writhed his arms out from under the straps of his combat pack, grunting as he knelt beside it to open the flap and withdraw the satellite phone. Then he palmed a second item from the same pouch, something metallic that he quickly stuffed into his pants pocket.

"Come on," he said, struggling to his feet. "Ditch the pack; we'll need all the speed we can manage. Break time's over."

* * *

Lightheaded, I trudged forward, wistfully dreaming of the moment when I could plop down and savor two minutes off my feet.

The heat was taking its toll in full—my brain felt like it was boiling in my skull. Within a few miles, I was completely incoherent and shuffling along over the scrub brush as the last of my sweat oozed from a dwindling reservoir in my body. It felt like we were fighting our way through an oven from which there was no escape. My left boot came untied, and as I watched the laces bouncing, I murmured, "One fucking job to do, is that too much to ask?"

"What?" Jais asked.

Every inch of ground passed painfully, slow beyond comprehension. Breathing was like sucking oxygen from a hairdryer.

There were no visible clouds and yet the sun descended into a murky crimson haze well above the horizon, its image rippling with heat as if it were being washed away by ocean waves. At times, everything went blurry.

I had to blink hard, restoring clarity for a minute before the dissolution of my surroundings repeated.

I was obsessed with the thought of water.

I kept reaching for a drinking hose that wasn't there, having left it behind inside my combat pack miles earlier. Then I'd feel pangs of remorse for abandoning a water supply, that there was somehow liquid remaining and a mere kink in the hose had stopped the flow. I dreamed up forgotten bottles of water stashed in my pockets; I patted down my chest rig over and over for some hidden vessel filled with liquid.

Instead I found AK magazines, now useless bricks suspended across my chest that would, at best, allow us to die in a blaze of glory.

My face began to go dry, feeling hot and flushed and soon without a drop of sweat to show for it. I said, "All the water in the world last night when we didn't want it. And not a shot glass full when we need it most."

Jais said nothing. He was walking sluggishly now, still limping forward with resolution, but his steps were becoming sloppy and aberrant. I was doing no better, save the limp, and had twice caught myself drifting far off course and veering east for no reason other than the delirium pounding my brain.

Our pace trickled to a staggering gait as we closed within three miles of our landing zone. When Jais collapsed for the third time, it wasn't with a scream of profanity or even a grunt. He just slammed into the ground on his left side and lay there, motionless.

I turned in a slow circle, scanning the darkening landscape in all directions.

The vegetation had thinned to nothing but barren scrub brush. There was no place to hide, no way to conceal our tracks. I thought of dying out here, alone in the desert, beside the man who was supposed to mentor my debut in the Outfit. Then I thought of my former team, and Karma.

Ophie's words returned to me. *It's all random and meaningless, boy, and I think you know that much by now.*

It didn't matter anyway.

The Indian had been wrong about nearly everything, and whether Ian had been acting as his puppeteer or not seemed almost beside the point. I had left the Dominican Republic with the sole purpose of killing the

Handler, and the resulting journey couldn't have taken me further from my goal.

I was now uncertain whether Ian was the betrayer or, barring that, if there had ever been a betrayal at all. I couldn't care less at present, while standing next to a collapsed partner on the far side of the world. We had a much greater chance of death by any number of factors than getting the case we sought, much less returning to America, both of which were now a distant afterthought to the simple ecstasy of a glass of tap water.

Walking to Jais, I set down my rifle and rolled him onto his back. His eyes were open, and through the exhaustion I could see a deep shame within them.

"You need to keep moving," he said, his voice raspy. "Three miles. Get the case."

Reaching under his shoulders, I propped him up to a sitting position. Then I sat behind him and leaned my back against his, achieving an uneasy equilibrium until I shifted my weight to compensate for his immense size.

I breathed a sigh of relief, the feeling of sitting on the hard-packed Somali desert as comfortable as a mattress of any price.

Grabbing my rifle, I set it atop my lap. I faced north and he south as we sat back-to-back with the sun setting beside us.

Finally, I said, "Not leaving you alone out here."

"Send someone back for me."

"Militia would get you before that. You've got the satellite phone...tell them we can't make it any farther."

"That's worse than the militia. Keep moving. Get the case. That's an order."

"Almost a hundred miles. Nonstop. Through this...shithole. We can rest a minute. That's my order."

"We're going to get killed here."

"Jais."

"What."

"How did you catch me?"

"Huh?"

"Last night. In freefall."

I felt him lean back his head as he replied, "Goddamned sky ninja."

I tried to laugh, but the air felt trapped in my chest. "You are."

"What happened with that...Somali? On the road."

"Dunno what you mean."

"Staring at that body. I had to walk over and...shake you out of it. On the road."

"Grenade blast. Rang my bell."

"Liar."

I asked, "What's in the case?"

He was quiet for a long time after that. Then I heard him exhale wearily. "The key to war."

"What?"

He dry-heaved twice, and then all was silent.

"Jais?"

No response.

"Jais?"

Hearing nothing, I leaned my head back against his, painfully closed my sun-scorched eyes, and had a sudden vision of him being escorted to meet the Handler upon our return from Somalia.

I saw Jais walking down a long hallway ending in a single door. It was flanked by twin men in suits, their hands hanging open at their sides in the manner of all bodyguards. As Jais approached, one reached for the handle and pushed open the door to reveal a long black desk centered before a high-back chair that faced the opposite direction. More guards emerged to stop and frisk Jais, who waited patiently until they were done. Jais proceeded forward, coming to a stop before the desk.

The chair slowly rotated to face him, revealing a slim white man seated comfortably. He wore a dress shirt with cuffs rolled two turns up lean forearms, and his eyes calmly appraised Jais behind the clear lenses of frail eyeglass frames. Delicate veins stood out on either side of his forehead.

Ian.

Before my thoughts could continue, I lapsed into a dark and weighted sleep.

* * *

When I woke up, the world was on fire.

My eyes scraped open to a blazing inferno sky of blood orange. I floated above the earth, my body as weightless as if it were sinking inside the steel drum, my senses warped to the ragged edge of functionality.

I saw my surroundings moving, was vaguely aware of shadows around me, though I felt nothing. Hands grasped at my body, lifting me upward as a rush of lightheadedness swept over me. My feet dragged behind me as I was pulled along the dirt, and despite my best efforts I couldn't recall where I was or what I was doing there.

The view darkened suddenly as I felt my weight being supported by some kind of surface beneath me. Although I could observe a peculiar play of light upon the indiscernible space, I soon lost my vision altogether.

A thin circle was pressed to my cracked lips, and I felt, for what seemed like the first time in my life, the rejuvenating flow of warm water into my mouth.

The circle vanished, and I weakly tried to grab for it. An eternity later it returned again, allowing me to take one sip before disappearing once more.

The cycle continued, with periodic sips punctuated by intervals of panic where I searched for the source of life like a newborn reaching for its mother's breast. But the process kept occurring, and gradually the drinks of water occurred between sips of a salty liquid I couldn't identify.

This occurred for perhaps a dozen repetitions, until one particular sip had the effect of none preceding it—in a split second, I was weighted, conscious, and sensing that I was sitting upright in the interior of a vehicle speeding over bumpy terrain.

With a rush of fear, I realized I was in Somalia and had been captured.

My eyes were covered with cloth, and I groped at the blindfold until two hands took mine to stop me.

"Jais!" I yelled, frantic with newly regained urgency. "Jais!"

Then I heard Jais's unmistakable voice beside me sounding as calm as always.

"David. Leave your blindfold on. We made it."

The hands lowered mine to my waist and then let go. The plastic circle pressed against my lips once more. I gratefully inhaled a pull of water before it disappeared again.

A deep, elderly male voice carved by the African continent said, "My friend, drink too fast and you will die. Allow me to help."

"Who are you?"

The man's voice sounded both assured and grateful, with a trace of humor lingering beneath the surface. "I am Elnaya. We have been looking for you for some time. You are now under the protection of the Silver Widow."

SALVATION

Altissima quaeque flumina minimo sono labi

-The deepest rivers flow with the least sound

10

The blindfolds remained over our eyes for the entire journey. This precaution amused me to no small end—for hours prior to our rescue, we saw no distinguishing features other than endless desert and scattered bones anyway.

As soon as I heard Jais's voice, my concern immediately returned to hydration. My mind was now somewhat restored by the endless succession of measured amounts of water and the unidentifiable salty liquid.

I felt my wrists, discovering that my watch and GPS had been removed. "How's your leg doing, buddy?" I asked Jais.

"Better now. How you holding up?"

"Starting to feel like myself. But I wish that—"

Elnaya interrupted, "My friends, save your strength. You may begin to eat a little now. When we arrive, you will get a proper meal. Until that time, remain silent and rest."

Two rough hands placed a small triangular shape into my palm. It smelled like a pastry, and I took a cautious nibble.

A cacophony of flavors exploded onto my palate, spiced meats and vegetables giving way to onions and potatoes in the single most amazing bite of food I have taken before or since.

Stuffing the rest into my mouth, I held out my hand for more but only received them rarely, and one at a time, between sips of water. Our vehicle crossed from the uneven desert surface to a smoother passage on what felt like a dirt road before returning to more uneven terrain.

I determined that we were sitting inside a vehicle that, judging by the noise, was a manual transmission, 8-cylinder diesel. The truck was large, which I could discern from the cumbersome creaking and the swaying as much as from the seating capacity—only Elnaya's voice addressed us, but I heard at least three other men either clearing their throats or quietly conversing in Somali.

The smell within the truck wasn't body odor, per se, but a strange and pungent scent that could only come from the bodies of men. It was a thick, smoky, woody scent, as if clothes had been baked in musky incense and then worn unwashed for days on end.

After much water and a little food, my body suddenly and deeply craved sleep. Within seconds of my mind lapsing into this groggy state of consciousness, I passed out.

When I came to, the vehicle was still moving, and I felt the weight of Jais's broad head resting on my shoulder. I fell back asleep and then awoke an indeterminate amount of time later to find myself slumped against him.

We stopped only once, when I awoke with a bladder that felt like it was about to rupture and said so.

The truck rumbled to a stop, and as soon as the engine fell silent I could hear a discord of birdcalls outside. Jais and I were helped out of the vehicle and led a short distance away to pee, and I could smell the humidity and hear the chatter of stationary birds coming from above that indicated tall trees. As we were led back to the vehicle, I thought I recognized the rush of moving water, but it was too faint to know for sure before the engine started again and our drive continued.

Several sips of water, a few more pieces of food, and I slept again.

* * *

At our journey's end, I wasn't sure if I was awake or asleep, only that I felt the truck coming to a stop. I heard vehicle doors opening and Elnaya's throaty voice saying, "Please, come with me." Jais's weight vanished from the seat beside me before I felt hands on my arm, guiding me sideways.

I was helped out of the vehicle and onto a sandy surface. I saw dim traces of light beneath my blindfold but was unsure whether it was radiating from sunlight or flame. A hand remained on my arm, and I followed its gentle forward pull, taking small, shuffling steps to places unknown.

The surface beneath my feet changed from sand to stone as the air around me became cooler. Footsteps echoed in front of me as I was led down eight steps. The hand turned me left and then forward again until it brought me to a stop, releasing my arm altogether. Footsteps shuffled on a dusty surface, and then I heard the dull bang of a heavy door closing behind me. The sound echoed broadly as if we were in a large, enclosed space.

Then my blindfold was removed.

I squinted amid the sudden light, blinking to adjust my eyes as I looked left to see Jais hunched beside me, his wrists also bare of his watch and GPS. He looked me up and down before we began examining our surroundings.

We stood on one side of a square room lit only by torches mounted on stone walls that were ornately engraved with primitive-looking symbols I didn't recognize as the script of any language.

In the center of the room, a circle of food platters and clay pitchers were arranged on the floor around a single delicate tree with a crooked, slender trunk that supported bursts of small green leaves.

Each wall bore a single door of a different color: green to my left, crimson to my front, and black to my right. I turned around to see Elnaya looking back at me with a slight grin, his featherweight body draped in a simple white tunic and loose red pants tarnished with dust.

He was an elderly man with bizarrely childlike eyes set deeply above wide cheekbones and a sparse white beard tightly curled and cropped close. His face was withered and dark, and his expression assumed a quiet dignity that seemed to regard Jais and me as unfortunate travelers he was compelled to help.

"My friends," he said, "eat a proper meal now. We have a banquet for you." As he spoke, his Adam's apple bobbed slowly on a thin neck draped in loose skin.

Jais nodded graciously. "Sir, we thank you for your hospitality. With your permission, I would like to speak with her."

He frowned slightly. "She is resting. Please, eat now."

Without waiting for argument, Elnaya turned and exited through a white door behind him. As it swung shut, Jais stepped forward to check the dull brass handle but found it locked.

He looked at me with a raised eyebrow.

I strode around the right perimeter of the room. My eyes drifted upward to find a small dome in the ceiling that hung directly over the feast, its concave surface crowned with a gold disc. Looking down, I checked the thick brass handle of the black door. Finding it locked, I followed the wall to the crimson door at the far side of the room before confirming it too was locked. When I looked up, Jais was turning away from the green door with a mournful shake of his head.

I shrugged and said, "Let's eat."

We walked to the food and stiffly lowered ourselves to the floor. I painfully arranged my shins until I was sitting cross-legged while Jais extended his left leg straight out beside me. The platters were piled high with yellow rice, chunks of meat, biscuits, and cakes. There were no utensils, and instead I grabbed a plate and used my hands to heap an assortment of food onto it.

Jais did the same while saying in a low voice, "I don't like this. Any of it."

I ripped off a length of flatbread, using it to roll a mass of rice and meat before biting off a chunk. The meat was unmistakably goat, but far better seasoned than I'd ever tasted while on deployment.

I swallowed. "Not to contradict you, boss, but I like this a whole lot better than our previous situation."

"Why would they lock us in here?"

"Who cares? Our orders were to do whatever they said, and they say to sit here and eat, so I'll sit here and eat. Besides, if they wanted to kill us they could have done it without herding us into Somali Disneyland."

I looked up again at the golden disc on top of the dome, now seeing that the blue space around it was painted with hundreds of tiny birds in flight, each moving in the same direction to form an endless swirl.

I asked, "How long do you think we were in that truck?"

"No idea. I slept through most of it."

I whispered, "We searched satellite imagery for hundreds of miles in every direction of the landing zone trying to see where they'd take us. There wasn't anything with a domed roof. Hell, I don't think there were many structures as big as this one room."

He nodded to the center of the banquet. The small tree rose from a stone pot lined with a neat row of symbols resembling those on the wall: vertical shapes made up of lines, circles, and crescents connecting in odd geometric patterns unlike anything I'd ever seen.

Then he said, "The script on that pot and these walls is pre-Islamic. You can bet we're off the beaten path for it to have survived this long. And you may want to be careful with eating that meat, my friend."

Chewing another mouthful of goat, I replied, "Eh. We'll be back to the land of antibiotics before any of this hits me."

Jais pinched salt from a small bowl and rained it over his plate. Then he offered me the bowl. I shook my head, instead filling two clay cups with tea from a tin kettle.

We picked up our respective cups and toasted each other, the brittle clay clinking together hollowly.

"To victory," Jais said.

"To victory," I repeated, taking a sip that tasted of honey and jasmine. "Your leg good to go now?"

"Better, yeah. I was more worried about the dehydration."

"You and me both. I needed the first few sips of water to put me back on planet earth."

"Me too."

"If they hadn't found us there—"

"They did," he cut me off. "Everything was shot to hell, but we made it. Now we have to get what we came for."

I nodded. "So be honest with me, Jais. On a scale of one to ten, where does this foray rank in terms of difficulty?"

His eyes were distant as he took a sip of tea and then lowered the cup to his lap.

"This is an easy seven. But most of the people who see eight and beyond come home in body bags, so don't get too jealous."

I inhaled deeply through my nostrils and let out the breath. I couldn't see any vents, but the still air in the room was clean. And there was more food arranged on the floor than Jais and I could put a dent in. After eating more than our fill to compensate for our trek across the open desert, the platters still looked like they hadn't been touched.

Jais suddenly asked, "What were you starting to say back in the desert, just before our booby-trapped truck exploded?"

My eyes ticked downward. "I'm not sure."

"Something about last summer. After your discharge."

The white door flew open with a loud clang, and I looked up expecting to see the aged figure of the Silver Widow.

Instead, Elnaya walked hurriedly toward us.

Jais somehow seemed to rise effortlessly, while I rolled onto all fours and stiffly transitioned my standing weight onto swollen knees.

Elnaya strode with youthful efficiency as he said, "My friends, we have two rooms for you. Rest now until she is ready."

Jais nodded diplomatically. "Sir, thank you again for your hospitality. But it is very urgent that we see her as soon as possible."

"Please," Elnaya said, "it is a dishonor to deny rest to travelers. You will go to your rooms until she summons you. This is our custom."

Then he touched Jais's arm and nodded to the green door, then led him there as I remained in place, watching them. Elnaya procured a set of keys, unlocked the door, and guided Jais inside.

When Elnaya reemerged, he closed the door and locked it from the outside. He walked to the opposite wall, circling the banquet before unlocking the black door and extending a hand to me.

"Thank you," I said, giving him a nod. He remained silent, but his wide eyes watched mine as I passed him, the irises appearing wet and black under the torchlight.

I entered a much smaller room lit by a single torch in the corner. The floor was covered in ornate carpet and lined with a variety of large pillows, and an adjoining doorway led to a toilet chamber consisting of a hole in the floor.

The door closed and locked behind me, leaving me alone. I glanced around the featureless stone walls, incredulous that, while on the brink of delirium during our desert passage, I had almost told Jais the truth about my past with Boss's team.

The urge to be completely honest with another human being, to break the walls of the impossibly dense maze that compartmentalized my life into oblivion, seemed to grow stronger every day since my separation from Karma. I wondered if I would ever be able to tell anyone the truth; maybe someday I'd have the opportunity to confide in some ally encountered along the way who desired the same end for the Handler that I did.

But that person would never be Jais.

He was simultaneously my friend and mentor, a born leader to whom my allegiance was unwavering. But his loyalty to the Handler was a far more dominating force, one that I could not, would not, break. Were our paths to cross again—me on a journey to harm the Handler and Jais on a mission to serve him—I had no doubt that Jais would have to kill me, or vice versa. There could be no other outcome.

With eyes growing heavy from food and the long journey, I lowered myself to the floor and unfolded my limbs to ease the pressure on my joints. I took a weary breath and arranged a pillow behind my head, grateful for the respite from events spanning a freefall over the edge of the Indian Ocean to the sanctuary in which we were now protected from both the elements and the enemy.

Well-fed and on solid ground, I desperately wanted to close my eyes again. Folding my hands over my stomach, I felt my body sinking into the ground as the space around me went dark.

* * *

An eternal blackness flashed into whitewashed brilliance with a streak of lightning, the foaming crests of colossal waves revealing a single ship skewing sideways on the water. When the squalling heavens brightened again, the ship pitched and rolled violently until its splintered masts were submerged and the hull vanished under a crushing wave—

My head leapt off the pillow as I reached for a weapon that wasn't there, instead taking in my surroundings. My chamber looked exactly as it had when I departed consciousness, save the open doorway beside me.

In its space stood a slight female figure cloaked in a long scarlet and gold dress with a sash wrapped over one shoulder. Her face was concealed by an intricate headdress of interlocking silver pieces that flowed to a point well beneath her chin, leaving only her eyes exposed.

She turned and drifted away.

I was on my feet in seconds and moving to the doorway. The woman had already crossed the central room and was passing through the crimson door to my right. The other two doors—one we had entered through and one Jais presumably remained behind—were closed. The torches burned as before, swathing the main chamber in pools of light and shadow.

I quickly strode to the open doorway she had disappeared through. Beyond it stretched a narrow hallway dimly lit by a single torch at the far end. The woman's silhouette slipped through a door on the right. I crossed a surface of crumbling shale and followed her inside.

She was seated atop a circular pillow that faced an elevated silver tray. On its surface rested a long, dark object I couldn't make out.

The room was perfectly square and lit by rows of candles that ascended the side of one wall. It was warm, peaceful, and completely silent, and the air held a faint smell of woody incense. A long, low bed sat at the far end, its shape clouded under blankets bearing elaborate stitching.

Her head was bowed, her features still concealed behind the mask of shimmering, interconnected silver discs draped over her face like chainmail. Opposite the sash, her exposed arm revealed skin the color of ebony wood that was beset from shoulder to fingertips with intricate, interconnecting patterns of henna more detailed than any tattoo.

She said, "Close the door."

Her voice was so quiet I could barely hear it, her accent both African and something else I couldn't place.

I said, "I would like my friend to be present as well."

"Do you want the case?"

"Of course."

"Then you stay alone."

Frowning, I reached back and grasped for the door handle, pulling it shut while keeping my eyes on her. She lifted her right hand to the circular pillow on the opposite side of the silver tray.

"Sit."

I slowly approached and lowered myself onto the pillow. Settling into a loose cross-legged position, I folded my hands respectfully in my lap and faced her from a distance of three feet. I glanced at the tray between us, which held a long, narrow pipe with a stem gracefully curled into a delicate bowl. Beside the bowl lay three crudely carved wooden matches lined up in a neat row.

Her eyes appeared old and weathered in the flickering candlelight as she reached behind her head. Unlatching her headdress, she removed the mask to reveal a face not of age but vibrant youth.

Her complexion was as radiant and dark as night, and her ethnic Somali features showed no emotion as she sat perfectly still. High, sculpted brows arched over exotic, smiling eyes of tremendous depth. She must have been in her late teens, if that, far younger than even I was. She set the silver veil down beside her.

I smelled faint traces of fragrant lavender perfume as she reached toward the tray, delicately lifting the small bulb at the end of the pipe and placing its slender neck beside her lips. "Help me," she said.

Retrieving one of the matches from the tray, I struck it against the stone floor. The flame sparked to life, and I brought it smoothly to the open bulb of the pipe. I held it as she puffed until embers began to glow within and then shook the life out of the match.

She inhaled deeply, breathing out a long stream of smoke with a rich, velvety floral smell.

Then she held the pipe toward me.

"I don't smoke," I said.

"Then I do not give you the case."

I waited another second, and when she didn't withdraw the pipe I took it from her. Taking a small drag, I was surprised to find the sweet aroma tasted like sour licorice in my mouth. I let the smoke billow from my parted lips and then handed the pipe back.

She took another drag before handing it back to me. The smoke floated from her mouth as she said, "Once more."

I took a second puff, noting that her endlessly deep eyes were searching mine, as if waiting for some indication from me. Her sculpted lips assumed the faintest trace of a smile, and as I handed her the pipe, her warm hand grazed mine. Then she gently set the pipe atop the elevated silver tray, where a faint trail of smoke rose between us.

I waited for her to speak, my mind remaining perfectly clear as I breathed out the last of the smoke. When she offered nothing, I asked, "What now?"

She breathed deeply through her open mouth, which shifted into a smile.

"Now you see the case."

As the last word left her mouth, her dress blazed with a deep scarlet glow and appeared to float around her as if suspended underwater. A rippling tingle of lightheadedness bloomed in the front of my brain, but my body pulsed with luxurious warmth and contentment. I felt as airy as if I were hovering eight feet above the floor.

My upper body wavered slightly, yet my mind churned with a godlike sense of control.

She unhurriedly lifted the silver tray between us and set it to the side, revealing a rectangular shape covered in gold cloth. Grasping a corner of the fabric with the thumb and forefinger of one hand, she pulled it back to reveal the case.

I stared at it in awe.

The case, the object of my desire that was necessary for me to walk the unlit path toward the Handler, appeared more sublime than any priceless work of art in the outside world.

It was just under a foot and a half in length, perhaps nine inches wide, and five inches deep. The brushed metal frame was colored somewhere between silver and copper, and the space between each corner was finished in a dull, ridged black surface. The leather-wrapped handle was flanked by black clasps next to twin brass combination rollers both set to the numbers

629. I reached for it, finally placing my hand on its surface after a brutal journey to find it.

She fiercely slapped her henna-covered hand atop mine.

I looked up to find my surroundings had melted away.

Suddenly I was alone, floating amid an infinite blackness with a murky glow. Squinting, I realized I was watching a vision of myself seated at a desk in a darkened room. The only light came from the blank white screen of a laptop. Its cursor blinked in silence.

I watched my own form take a sip of bourbon from a glass to his left and then place both sets of fingertips over the keyboard.

He typed the words, *Relax. We all knew this was coming.*

Sitting back, satisfied, he reached once more for the bourbon before stopping abruptly. He briefly rested his hand in his lap before reaching into the shadows beside the computer and picking up the .454 revolver sitting on the desk.

A sigh of contentment, and then he put the barrel in his mouth and unceremoniously pulled the trigger.

The blast exploded around me, dissipating with a surreal echo as I startled, returning somehow to my seat in front of the case. Blinking my hazy vision clear, I looked across from me to find that the woman seated there was now Karma.

She appeared exactly as she had when I first saw her, with pale lipstick offset by pink-streaked blonde hair. The henna patterns of the Silver Widow's arms were replaced by the bright Koi fish and cherry blossoms etched into Karma's skin. Her petite, lithe body shifted as she raised one arm at the elbow, the smoke lazily drifting from a cigarette perched between her fingers as her clear blue eyes narrowed with the onset of a grin.

I gasped sharply, and she opened her mouth to say something, raising an assuring hand as my first stuttering blinks caused her to vanish from sight.

Now her features had transformed back into the young Somali woman, her hand still atop mine over the case.

She released my hand, and suddenly my mind was clear and her face had returned to its previous clarity. I looked around the room. Everything was exactly as before—the candles, the smell of incense, and the case on the floor between us.

She said, "Now I am glad I did not allow your friend here."

I was breathing quickly as though catching my breath after a sprint. "Why?"

"He is loyal to your employer."

"Yes. So am I."

She shook her head. "No, you want to recover the case."

"Of course I do. My friend and I have been through much danger to get it."

"No, you have not."

"I'm not sure you understand what it took for us to get here."

"I understand completely. You want to recover the case, but not because you serve your employer."

"Why else would I bring it back?"

"So you can draw a blade across his throat. Believe me, David Rivers, the danger is ahead of you, not behind."

A rush of fear surged through me. Was this another test?

I asked only, "Who are you?"

"I am the Silver Widow."

"The Silver Widow is old. Who are you?"

She gave a cold smile. "I am one who wants the same thing you do."

"Why?"

"*Why* does not matter. Let us concern ourselves with *how*."

"Then how?"

"You will tell them you met with a very old woman."

I shook my head. "If I get caught lying, neither of us will get what we want."

"She did not remove her mask."

"I have been assured he sees everything."

"She did not speak."

"I'll get killed."

"You might be killed, yes. But if you do not do as I say, it will happen before your first sunset in America. You do not grasp the danger you are in."

Leaning back, I watched her face for some further clue as to her intentions. I saw none.

Then I said, "I don't know when I will meet him. It may take a decade or more."

"We do not have a decade. A few years at best."

"Before what?"

"Before he discovers the truth."

"How?"

"It does not matter. You must meet him quickly. Do whatever it takes."

"Then help me."

"I am helping you. But you must also find a way."

I swallowed, tasting the fading smoke in my mouth. "What else can you tell me?"

"Giants are not slain at the end of golden roads."

"What?"

She gave a frustrated sigh. "If the opportunity to kill him seems certain, then do not proceed. He is going to test you, and when the moment seems perfect to complete your revenge, that is the very time you must not do it."

I nodded. "What do you get out of this?"

"That does not matter unless you succeed."

"And then what?"

"If you live, I will come calling and you will not forget my help. Now take your prize and go. Your friend is awake."

Grasping the case's handle, I carefully stood and felt its weight for the first time. I gauged it to be between forty and fifty pounds, just as Jais had said.

I looked at her seated figure. "I want to doubt you, but I don't think I have a choice."

In that moment, lit by the undulating candlelight, she appeared for a fleeting second as Laila—strawberry-blonde hair, electric green eyes, the face, the curves, and everything in between.

So too did her voice match Laila's as she said, "We all get a choice, David."

I blinked hard, twice, trying to clear the smoke's effects from my mind.

The young Somali woman was in place as before, though she no longer watched me.

Instead she reached down and lifted the silver mask, draping it over her face and fastening it behind her head. The henna-covered arms lowered to her waist, and suddenly she appeared very old once again, staring into oblivion as if I had never entered the room.

I turned, opened the door, and walked back down the hall, the heavy case suspended in my left hand.

* * *

I turned the handle of the crimson door and pushed it open to enter the main chamber.

As I let it swing shut behind me, I saw Jais pacing under the golden dome.

"I got it," I said breathlessly.

His eyes fixed on me, then the case in my hand, and then back to my face.

He said, "Where have you been?"

I lifted the case. "Getting this. I was only gone a few minutes."

"Really? Because I've been waiting here for hours." He strode past me and tested the door handle. Upon finding it locked, his jaw clenched.

Then he turned to me, reaching into a pocket with one hand and clasping my left arm with the other.

By the time I saw the glint of silver metal and realized what he was doing, it was too late. As I tried to recoil, he snapped one handcuff over my wrist and latched the other around the handle of the case.

"What the fuck are you doing?" The hair on the back of my neck stood up as a turbulent mix of rage and fear swirled within me. My mind returned to the night I was handcuffed to the pipe in the basement while Cancer tortured me.

Jais's expression remained unmoved. "I have my orders, too. And these aren't coming off until we get home."

"How am I supposed to shoot a weapon like this?" I said.

"How am I supposed to go to my meeting when I get back? What can I say about the Silver Widow—that I never saw her?"

For the first time since I'd met him in the interview room at the Complex, I didn't know what to say. He whirled around and paced over to the white door on the opposite side of the room. I followed him numbly, casting a final glance at the small potted tree, the only marking that remained of our grand banquet.

Jais pounded on the door until it opened, revealing Elnaya calmly appraising us as if he had been waiting to be summoned.

Jais said, "We want to be delivered to our drop-off point shortly after nightfall to move under cover of darkness. Since I don't know what time it is, I need you to tell me when we can leave to make that happen."

"This is not possible," Elnaya said in a courteous tone, procuring the two blindfolds and holding them out to us. "You have completed your business, and now you must leave. The truck is waiting."

11

As the truck came to a stop, I pulled the strip of cloth off my head and squinted at the daylight and green vegetation outside my window. Jais was seated beside me but didn't meet my eyes as he opened the door and stepped out. From the passenger seat, Elnaya turned his head to watch me with an expression falling somewhere between sympathy and regret before he, too, exited.

As I slid the case along the seat and toward the door, three other guards in *shemaghs* got out with their weapons and formed a small perimeter around us, facing outward. I stepped onto solid ground, and my left arm assumed the full weight of the case that hung suspended from my hand.

I could tell at once that it was morning; the final traces of humidity from the previous night were still detectable in the air before the sun's wrath peaked in the afternoon hours.

Turning to catch a glimpse of the truck's exterior, I found a vintage, sand-colored Land Rover equipped with a brush guard, snorkel, and roof rack loaded with fuel cans and supplies. Then I looked at my surroundings, getting a ground view of the terrain that Jais and I would be moving over for the two-mile hike to our helicopter pick-up location.

We were standing on a dirt road representing the last vestige of flat ground, as the terrain to our north slanted upward into rolling foothills that increased in height. We were far from the barren desert wasteland we had encountered south of the landing zone—now, the hillsides were dotted with low green shrubbery interspersed with a number of boulders placed so curiously that it seemed to be intentional. A wide procession of shadows inching over the landscape heralded a flock of white clouds overhead, their movement ushered by an intermittent and welcome breeze washing over us from the west.

Elnaya swung open the tailgate mounted with two spare tires to reveal our confiscated equipment. Jais and I immediately took possession of the Galil rifles we hadn't seen since passing out in the desert and checked that they were loaded and chambered. Jais stuffed the satellite phone into a cargo pocket, and we turned on our GPS devices before donning chest rigs.

This last action was easier for Jais than me—with my left wrist still handcuffed to the case, I was forced to route it through the straps of my chest rig and then arrange the rest around my neck and opposite shoulder.

I strapped my watch on my right wrist and noted that the time was 10:32, the date December 31.

Elnaya spoke the first words since we had stopped. "We stand at the agreed drop-off to the east of Saakow. Do you agree?"

Jais consulted his GPS before replying, "I do."

With his hands clasped behind his back, Elnaya dipped his head sharply in a bow before raising it once more. "Very well. This ends her protection over your journey. Good luck, my friends."

The guards loaded into the vehicle, with Elnaya boarding last and settling into the passenger seat. As his door closed, a high-pitched chirping preceded the low, rumbling roar of the diesel engine firing to life.

Jais began walking immediately, threading his way up the shallow hillside in front of us. I followed him toward our helicopter pick-up site, glancing right to watch the Land Rover pull forward and accelerate down the dirt path, the twin spare tires watching me like eyes. The road wound past a hillock to our east, and the truck followed it, soon disappearing from view.

Jais's large frame now moved easily. He didn't speak, so neither did I, uncertain where his mood had settled since his outrage at seeing me with the case. Our shared silence continued for several minutes of uphill exertion, which was all the time it took for me to realize how long a two-mile hike could seem.

The case was an anchor. Its contents didn't shift or slide; instead, the entire mass felt like the uniform density of a bowling ball, which, together with the handcuff restriction, made it impossible to carry with the slightest degree of comfort.

I tried hefting the case into the crook of my right elbow and covering ground with my rifle slung the opposite direction, picking up my pace as we neared the high ground of the shallow slope.

"I'm sorry for snapping at you back there," Jais said abruptly.

I considered my words for a moment. "She didn't give me a choice, Jais. I tried to get you."

"What was she like?"

"Old. Like, really old."

"So what happened when you were in there?"

"Depends."

"On what?"

I cracked a smile. "Does the Outfit do random drug testing?"

He gave a mocking laugh. "No, but what happens on an Outfit op stays on an Outfit op. Doesn't mean you can keep secrets from me, so let's hear it."

"She made me smoke something."

"Oh, twisted your arm, did she?"

"I'm serious. She wouldn't show me the case until after I smoked a pipe."

"Weed?"

"No. I was seeing all kinds of stuff—she turned into an ex-girlfriend at one point. Really trippy shit."

"Then she gave you a hallucinogenic. Could have been any number of opiates or herbs."

"Why would she do that?"

"That's the million-dollar question. Did she ask you anything?"

"No. She didn't even talk, just gestured."

"Don't sweat it, David. Odds are this won't be the weirdest thing you do with the Outfit. And you did a bang-up job—don't think otherwise because of my lapse in professionalism. I'd work with you again any day."

I heaved the case behind my back, placing the weight on one shoulder blade as I replied, "Well I may not be much of a partner, but I'm a hell of a mule."

We crested a ridgeline and saw a descent ahead of us that eventually rose to a taller hilltop a quarter mile away.

Jais said, "This has been a rough ride, but it's your first trip out of the Complex and my responsibility is to set the standard of conduct by example. I owe that to the Outfit as much as to you."

"Lashing out I can handle. But why did you handcuff this thing to me?"

"I told you. I have my own orders."

"You could have waited until we got a little closer to the pick-up site. I wouldn't have told anyone, I promise you." I returned to the straight-arm carry as my left arm fell asleep.

"There are no shortcuts in this business, David. If you remember nothing else I've taught you, remember that."

* * *

We began ascending another hill, its boulder-lined crest appearing an eternity away.

I glanced at the handcuffs on my left wrist, casting my thoughts onto what other orders Jais may have that I wasn't privy to. If he hadn't mentioned the handcuffs until after he'd slapped them on me, then what else awaited us as the mission dwindled down to completion and we boarded our flight to the Complex? The Somali woman, whoever she was, told me I wouldn't survive the following sunset if I didn't heed her advice. If that was true, I had a hard time believing that Jais wasn't aware on one level or another.

He said, "So are you going to tell me now what you were about to say in the desert?"

I hesitated as the black shape of an enormous bird of prey soared alongside us, slightly above eye level. As it glided above our heads, the curvature of its wings trembled and adjusted to the breeze.

I said, "What do you think the wingspan on that thing is?"

"Don't change the subject."

"It was just something stupid. When I was hiking the Smoky Mountains—"

A sharp *crack* sounded against the boulder beside me. The case hit the ground, its weight almost pulling my shoulder out of its socket. I slammed down beside it before I had time to flinch. I had reacted before consciously realizing the sound was a bullet strike.

Jais fell prone in front of me as the echo of a single high-pitched gunshot rippled over the hills.

"You all right?" he asked, sliding toward me on his elbows.

"Yeah. Sniper?"

"Dragunov shot. It came from the east, so we need to swing to the west side of this hill. Get above him on the high ground and then find an alternate route to the pick-up site. Let's go."

As he began high-crawling around a boulder, I called after him, "Easy for you to say—you don't have a fucking anvil chained to your arm."

"Baby steps, Rivers," he yelled back.

I followed him as best I could, pushing the case ahead of me and using it to pull myself up the hill with the Galil still lodged in the crook of my free arm.

Once we made it to the opposite side of the boulder, Jais rose to his feet and darted to the next cluster of rocks. I waited for him to arrive and then followed suit. Another bullet glanced off stone somewhere to my right as I crashed into his side behind cover.

We stayed as low as we could, bounding between rocks to the west side of the hill, away from the sniper. A final shot rang out before we separated ourselves from his view altogether, though I couldn't hear where it impacted as we continued moving uphill toward a vantage point where we could reappraise our route.

Unencumbered by the case, Jais disappeared over the crest and onto the hilltop minutes before I did.

I struggled uphill with panting breaths, my left arm screaming for relief from the dead weight pulling it toward the earth. At any moment I expected

Jais to yell down to me, his words surely consisting of some good-natured ridicule bemoaning my lack of speed.

Instead, I heard the low murmur of his voice.

By the time I crested the terrain, I saw he was holding the Iridium satellite phone to his ear with its antenna angled skyward.

"...now read that location back to me," he said.

I crouched and moved forward, pointing my rifle north and scanning the ground with my magnified optic.

I made out the shape of a vehicle six hundred meters away that was passing between the hills and stopping to let out armed men at varying intervals. It wasn't a pickup like the one we had driven but rather a larger flatbed that appeared to be loaded with fighters.

Jais said into the phone, "I confirm, that is our current location. Request immediate extraction."

Shifting my view to the east, I saw a second truck dropping off men who quickly assembled into patrol formations and began approaching us on foot. Then a third truck stopped to the west. The vehicles were circling our position and dismounting fighters just out of range for us to accurately engage with our Galils.

Once the enemy closed the distance between us on foot, we would run out of ammunition long before they did.

I scanned the south and saw a fourth truck stopped on the dirt road we had walked in from, its men already released into the countryside to hunt us.

"I copy all," Jais continued. "But understand that we are surrounded. Unable to maneuver. Have visual on five enemy vehicles, estimate four-zero enemy personnel in total. That may be too long. Yes, I confirm."

He pressed a button on the phone, pushed the antenna down, and looked at me. "Welcome to the Alamo."

I knelt beside the case. "What about the helicopter?"

"Mechanical issues. ETA is an hour and a half." I started a countdown timer on my watch as he continued, "Get into position facing south. I'll cover the north. Our sectors of fire are 180 degrees. All we have to do is hold them off until our bird gets here."

I moved to the southwest side of the hilltop and looked through my optic at another truck releasing its men.

I called back to him, "Jais, these are off-road flatbed trucks, not pickups with machineguns. And the dismounts are moving in tactical formations instead of rushing to their deaths. I don't think these are the same people we dealt with south of the landing zone."

"They're not."

"Then why are they after us?"

He paused. "They're not after us; they're after the case. Just focus on the enemy, David. We've got to make our ammo last, so don't waste it on anything over five hundred meters away. Remember, we're only outgunned as long as we're missing."

"Yeah, I got that," I said, settling into the prone position and readying my rifle from behind the cover of a boulder.

Then I stopped, feeling the breeze that carried with it the rolling clouds sweeping over the hills around us, my mind inexplicably plagued by some notion I couldn't put my finger on. Brushing it aside as pre-gunfight nerves, I returned my eye to the optic.

The first group of men I saw were traveling in a loose wedge, patrolling cautiously at a distance of 550 meters. Close enough, I thought, leveling the appropriate tick mark below the crosshairs of my sight on the center man in the formation.

I fired three rounds, watching carefully for the outcome and seeing it when the group scrambled behind cover.

A single incoming bullet barked off the stone to my front. I slid behind it and began crawling to the other side of the rock cluster, dragging the case alongside me as Jais began firing on the opposite side of the hilltop.

Now angled to the southeast, I searched for targets and settled on another group closing inside of five hundred meters, rounding the base of a foothill and moving quickly toward us. I shot two more rounds, seeing one of their number stumble and get dragged behind cover as I chased his rescue party with another three bullets.

Once again, a single round slapped into the rock I was hiding behind.

I called to Jais, "That Dragunov is still out there! I'm getting some near misses."

He shot twice and then yelled back, "There's one on my side too. He's almost tagged me a few times now."

I slid the case through the dirt and crawled behind a rock facing east; Jais did the same on his side of the hilltop. No one was moving through my optic, but I found a pair of heads peering over a small berm. Not wanting to waste my crawl over the rocky ground, I shot twice before moving back to face the south.

Jais suddenly yelled, "Stop shooting!"

"What's wrong?"

Another sniper round pinged off the rocks beside me.

Jais said, "They've stopped advancing on my side. See if they're getting any closer on yours."

I crawled to another cluster of rocks, sweeping the low ground with my optic. "No, I don't see any movement."

"That's what I was afraid of."

I thought for a moment. "You think they've got a mortar?"

"I'd be surprised if they didn't—these aren't your average Somali militia, David. We're dealing with something else."

"If they were going to hit us with indirect fire, they would have done it by now."

"No, they would much prefer to take us alive. But they're not going to wait all day and lose half their men doing it. They must know by now we've got a helicopter on the way."

"Aren't they afraid of blowing up the case?"

"A regular explosion isn't going to destroy what's inside. They can pull it out of the ashes for all they care. But we've got to stay put. If we move from this hilltop, the snipers will get us. If we stay, at least we've got a shot of surviving the mortars long enough for the helicopter to get here."

I shook my head. "If they don't get a hit on the first try, it's not going to take them long to adjust fire until they do."

At this, we heard the distant *thump* of a mortar tube firing somewhere to the southeast.

The first round was airborne, beginning the parabolic arc that would carry it to its detonation against the earth. I realized that I was now on the receiving end of the same weapons system I had been tasked with employing to attack the Five Heads on my final mission with Boss's team.

Jais and I scrambled to our respective rock clusters, and I slipped between the biggest boulders I could find. Looking out of the narrow opening, I saw Jais similarly huddled between stones rising to shoulder height above his crouched form.

"We only have to survive a few mortar rounds," he said. "As soon as they think we're dead, they'll charge in to get the case before the helicopter gets here. We'll let them get too close to use their mortar and then start killing them again."

"Great plan, Jais, provided we survive the fucking mortars in the first place."

"Baby steps, Rivers."

The mortar round exploded behind me, and the quick reverberation of the earth and our boulders jolted us before the sound receded into an echo sweeping away from us like the tide.

I called, "Sounds like a 60-millimeter. Landed maybe 150 meters to the south."

"More like two hundred meters. Let's see how long it takes them to—"

Another *thump* of the mortar firing.

"—adjust fire."

I said, "Well I don't hear a fucking helicopter coming, so I hope this case is worth dying over. You may as well tell me what's in it."

"You must have figured it out by now."

"Judging by weight, I'm guessing uranium."

"Not just uranium. We could cross the border into Uganda and find mines filled with uranium."

The second mortar round exploded with a louder blast than the first, but this time the sound came from my front, on the opposite side of the hill —they were bracketing us and would be making progressively smaller adjustments to the mortar's aim until they achieved a direct hit.

Jais continued, "The billet in that case was refined in a centrifuge at Novosibirsk. It was sold in Ukraine in 2004—"

There was another distant blast as the third mortar round shot out of the tube.

"—and then went missing as it crossed the Black Sea to Turkey. It showed up for sale in Yemen last month, open to the highest bidder."

I looked at the case chained to my wrist. "If he could afford it, then why did we have to jump in to get it?"

"Because everyone who couldn't afford it has been looking for it. There's only one place in this part of the world to keep something like that hidden, and that's where he sent us."

The third round detonated once again on the south side of the hill, so close that the deafening explosion was replaced by dirt raining over our heads.

I cringed with the impact. "So the Handler wants to build a bomb. That's what you meant when you said it was the key to war."

We heard a fourth round being fired, and I knew in that instant that it would hit the hilltop.

Jais was now yelling, "He didn't send us so he could build a bomb with it; he sent us so no one else could. That's why we have to hold these fuckers off until the helicopter gets here. If we don't get the case out, the contents are going to be weaponized to the full abilities of whoever gets ahold of it. And they're going to save it until they can get it into a population center or next to—"

He was interrupted by a thunderbolt that split the sky and turned the world around us to blackness.

* * *

I heard the Indian's voice in my head, his words as clear as they were during our meeting in the forest.

You tell me, David. How does one escape an enemy such as this?

Then I was painfully descending the narrow staircase at the team house the day after I killed Saamir, banished from the dining room meeting where Boss, Matz, and Ophie were deciding my fate. Two doors at the bottom of the steps, the one on the right leading to my room and the one on the left leading to the cellar where—

"*AMSAKTUH! KABADTO ALAYH!*"

The words, shouted from mere feet away, were met with the sound of dozens of men cheering from farther down the hill.

I opened my eyes to see Jais's motionless, bloody body sprawled on the ground between boulders.

My vision shifted to the Galil rifle lying two feet from my outstretched hand. I made a desperate scramble to grab it only to see a tan boot kick it away.

I rolled onto my side, squinting into the light at a tall, well-built Arab brandishing an AK-47.

He was the first enemy fighter to have made it atop the hill. We faced each other, alone. Through a ringing head, I listened in vain for the drumming beat of helicopter blades approaching from the distance.

Instead, I heard the man speaking with a thick Middle Eastern accent. "It is over. You are prisoner now."

I lowered my head back to the dirt and released a shaky exhale.

"Get up," he said.

Pressing a palm to the ground, I struggled to rise to my hands and knees. He crudely grabbed the back of my shirt, jerking me upward as I stumble-stepped to a crouched, bent-over position, the weight of the case upsetting my perilous equilibrium. I grabbed the handle tightly with both hands, trying to steady the momentum of the case before I toppled over.

Then I inhaled as deeply as I could.

Channeling all my strength into a single movement, I swung the case upward with both hands.

It moved with surprising speed, striking the side of the man's head with a sickening *pop*. He spun a full rotation as he fell to the ground, landing on his back with his vacant eyes facing the clouds.

The Indian's voice filled my head once more, though I had no idea why.

He is many things to many people.

I fell to my knees beside the body, raising the case over my head with both hands and bringing it down like a sledgehammer onto his face.

To his workers, he is the Handler.

I heaved the case away from the carnage and extended both arms above my body as high as I could reach. Then I swung it back down.

To his inner circle, he is the One.

As I lifted the case again, I saw that the remains of the human head looked as Karma's did at the moment of her death, a gruesome display within pieces of fractured skull. Raising the case as high as I could, I flung it downward a final time.

To his enemies, he is—

"*KHASHAM KHADA!*" I screamed, as loud as my lungs would allow. "*KHASHAM KHADA! KHASHAM KHADA!*"

Voices on the hill below began yelling in another language. Their chattering cries echoed from man to man down the hill and then reversed course as a garbled phrase was repeated back up in the form of an instruction.

A second enemy fighter emerged onto the hilltop, then a third, their AK-47s maintaining vigil on my figure as they surveyed the scene.

Still on my knees, I panted in exhaustion, the case now on the ground beside the dead man's destroyed skull as I muttered, "*Khasham Khada...Khasham Khada* sent me, you motherfuckers..."

To my left I saw the cratered earth where the mortar round had impacted, charring the surrounding rocks into chimneys of black. Half a dozen fighters climbed onto the hilltop, directing their barrels toward me but saying nothing as they kept their distance. I saw both Somalis and Arabs among their ranks, the vengeance in their eyes intensifying the longer they stood, sweaty hands tightening on the wood grips of their assault rifles.

Then, without warning, their ranks parted.

Through the gap came a slight man whose shuffling passage caused the fighters to spread further. Alone, he limped toward me, a checkered *shemagh* tied around the top of his head with the excess hanging across the front of one shoulder. His left hand deftly maneuvered a cane as he walked, his only armaments untouched on an embroidered leather belt: a dagger with an ivory handle in a curved sheath on one hip and a holstered pistol on the other.

I looked at him and said, "*Khasham Khada* will kill you all. *Khasham Khada.*"

He watched my eyes without speaking.

He must have been in his sixties, with every possible line and wrinkle carved into his stern, olive-skinned face. The lower half of his beard was dyed a bright orange-red, and though long and unkempt his upper lip had been neatly and recently shaved bare. After directing his gaze around the hilltop, he gave a barely discernable nod before tapping a low rock beside me with two quick raps of his cane.

The nearest fighters leapt forward to support his arms as he lowered himself into a seated position on the rock and set his cane gently across his lap with a dignified air.

I bluffed as convincingly as I could. "My helicopters will be here any second with three dozen men. You had better be gone before that happens."

He responded in an amused tone, with a crisp Middle Eastern accent that I couldn't quite place, "Only one helicopter has departed Mogadishu in the past hour." He swung his walking stick toward me, quickly setting the tip atop my right wrist with gentle precision. "And the timer on your watch is counting down from forty-seven minutes."

I looked down at my wrist, then back at him.

"Worth a shot."

He gave an appreciative nod. "It was a noble effort. Now let us talk. So there is no misunderstanding, what words have you been saying?"

"You know the words. *Khasham Khada.*"

"Yes, I do know those words. I also know that I was not informed of your passage through Somalia."

"Well I 'informed' as many of your soldiers as I could before you started shooting mortars. And the first man who made it over the hill was also well aware before his soul departed."

"I see that. But if you know these words, then you also know the man who armed you with them to ensure your safety."

"Of course."

"And you would also know that he would not send a mission under the protection of the words you just spoke without first informing all relevant parties. In this case, and in this part of the Caliphate, that would be me."

"Yet here I am. And your treatment of me will determine how well—or poorly—he responds to your interference."

The man flinched. "He is willing to risk all-out war? For this?" He gave the side of the case a tap with his stick. "It is valuable, but not that valuable. If he had simply told me he was the buyer, we would have avoided this mess altogether."

"I do not question the One. Do you?"

He paused to examine the rolling hills receding into the distance toward the ocean that lay too far over the horizon to see.

"Of course not. Have you...have you met him?"

"Yes. And I will be reporting to him immediately upon my return."

"Is he truly the luminary that the network would have us believe?"

I raised my eyes from his peculiar orange beard to meet his stare. "He is even greater than they say. His genius is decades ahead of its time."

He paused, glancing skyward with his mouth ajar, looking deep in thought. "Tell him...tell him I would like his people to contact Sasa at their earliest convenience. To discuss this matter."

I nodded. "I will relay your message, and if you grant one small request, I'll also tell him that my mission was treated with the utmost courtesy despite the misunderstanding."

"What is your request?"

"You leave me one AK-47 when you go."

His hands flexed on the cane, one sliding to the end before he replied, "A rifle? Why this of all things?"

"Mine has suffered a malfunction, and I wish to remain armed. Decide quickly, because if the men aboard my helicopter arrive to see me surrounded I cannot assure your safety."

He glanced back down at my watch and then yelled over his shoulder, "Carry the martyr and—"

Then, shaking his head in mild embarrassment, he switched to Arabic and relayed his orders.

The fighters around us didn't move for several seconds, at which point the man's face clouded with a dark convulsion of rage and he screamed, "*AL-AN!*"

The men scrambled to action, splitting into two groups. One recovered the body of their fallen friend, whose head was scattered about the Somali hilltop and smeared upon my case, and the others helped their leader to his feet as he spoke to them quietly. I took the opportunity to glance at his belt, noting that the embroidered pattern was Arabic calligraphy.

He turned to me. "Until we meet again."

I nodded. "Until then."

Then the fighters turned and left, descending the sloping terrain away from the hilltop. They began disappearing over the ledge, casting backward glances at me that ranged from naive curiosity to lingering anger at my survival.

The single AK-47 belonging to the dead fighter remained on the ground beside me, resting beside a patch of sand congealed with blood and brain matter.

As the last fighters vanished from the hilltop, I clambered to my feet and rushed to Jais, kneeling beside him and pressing two fingers into his neck.

* * *

He was alive, his pulse steady below the corner of his jaw.

The right half of his face was unmarred except for dirt and sweat, its expression appearing almost serene.

But the rest of his face was virtually unrecognizable.

His left eyelid was grossly swollen under a dark crimson thumbprint of a wound, the penetration serving as the source for a river of blood that flowed parallel to others streaming from his forehead, nostril, and the corner of his mouth.

Jais's other injuries were muted by the veneer of his clothes, his chest and shoulder peppered with an irregular red splatter as if a dripping paint-brush had been flung at him. Dozens of tiny pieces of shrapnel were embedded in his flesh. Yet he had survived a near-direct mortar impact through the absurd and unfathomable ballistics of the angle of its strike and his positioning among rock cover.

Had he ordered me to cover the north side of the hill, the injuries would have been mine, and the Indian's safeguarding words would have gone unsaid. Had the mortar been any system larger than a 60-millimeter, we both would have been killed on impact.

I stood and glanced at the countdown on my watch, recovering the abandoned AK-47 and checking that it was ready to fire. Then I searched the sky to the east but heard no trace of an inbound aircraft.

For a fleeting second, I was back on the staircase in Boss's team house, approaching two doors at the bottom of the steps. The one on the right still led to my room, and the one on the left still led to the cellar where Boss had first interrogated me.

And where Luka had been tortured and killed before my eyes.

I kicked Jais's rifle away from him and then swung the toe of my boot into his ribs.

He groaned and stirred, his right eyelid fluttering open as the left remained swollen shut. I stepped back and set the case atop a rock, then leaned the AK-47 over it to face him.

When Jais's eye opened fully, he came to life in a panic and looked around wildly for his rifle.

"They're gone," I said. Realizing he couldn't hear me, I yelled, "They're gone!" His eye found me and his expression softened somewhat.

"What happened?" he asked in a loud voice.

"What does *Khasham Khada* mean?"

"I can't hear you...my left ear is fucked..."

"*Khasham Khada*," I shouted. "What does it mean?"

"I have no idea."

"Me neither. But it turned all those fighters around as soon as their commander heard it."

He glanced at the stain of blood and brain matter in the sand, the last remaining trace of the fighter I'd killed with the case. "David, what happened?"

"It doesn't matter what happened. All that matters is what's about to."

"What?"

"You were wrong about one thing. Your team wasn't wiped out completely. There was a single survivor from their last mission."

He squinted in confusion. "You're not making any sense, David."

"Just like there's going to be a single survivor from this one."

I waited for recognition to pass over his face, and when it did, I saw his right eye searching again for a weapon on the ground beside him.

"Don't bother," I said. "You're not leaving this hilltop alive."

At this, a flurry of muscle movement rippled beneath his shirt. He planted one blood-smeared palm down, then turned onto his stomach to brace the other hand against the sand. Both arms flexed in a shuddering current of strength as he pushed himself to his knees, holding onto a boulder beside him to fight his way upward.

His left leg remained straight as he used his right leg to support his bodyweight, shuffling his foot sideways to lean his spine against the rock behind him.

The wounds on his face and body began a new purge of blood as he completed the effort and faced me with his open eye watching me coldly. "I don't know if that mortar impact hurt your brain or if you've just lost your mother*fuck*ing mind. But you've got one second to stop pointing that gun at me before I kill you where you stand."

I shouted back, "You said we'd only be outgunned as long as we were missing. The last person who told me that was Matz. I worked with him, and Boss, and Ophie. And Karma. None of them survived that day, and yet there's a survivor. That's how I know who you are."

The intense anger in his face melted away, yielding instead to unmistakable fear. He said nothing as I continued, "You had already left by the time I met them. They didn't call you Jais; they called you Caspian."

He didn't answer.

Instead, a deathly silence filled the void between us. I could practically see his mind racing to comprehend his predicament and find a way out. Before he spoke again, a stream of moments rushed through my memory.

The first time I'd heard Matz say Jais's name.

We're not a depression rehab center. And being down a man shouldn't be an excuse to keep everyone we bring in for a job. We're not getting Caspian back.

Ophie's words to Luka in the basement.

We know you killed Caspian. You're just here to answer for it.

Then Boss.

I had a dream right before Caspian got killed…

For the first time, I watched the man I knew as Caspian, now a wounded figure covered in blood and standing face-to-face with me on a hilltop on the far side of the world.

When he broke the silence, it was with a yell. "I didn't betray them!"

"And yet you're working for their killer."

"They were pushing it too far, David—every mission was riskier than the last, and it was only a matter of time before they knew too much for the Handler to let us retire. I tried to tell Boss a hundred times, but they wouldn't back down. There was no other way. They wouldn't let me leave. I had to make them think I was dead."

You tell me, David. How does one escape an enemy such as this?

I said, "I watched Ophie torture Luka to death for killing you."

"Luka was a traitor to his own—"

"I don't give a shit who your fall guy was, Caspian. Luka kept saying it wasn't him, that the Iranian killed you. That was your scout, wasn't it? In the desert I asked if Sergio recruited you. You said it was an Iranian named Roshan."

"David, listen to me," Jais said in an appeasing tone, using the back of his hand to wipe the blood flowing from his mouth. "My mom came down with ovarian cancer. It was stage four before they found it. I couldn't afford the treatments, not even with team money. He promised to take care of her, and he has. She's in the best facility with the best specialists in the world."

Karma's voice again, on the back porch.

Caspian went home to see his mom when she got her diagnosis and he disappeared within a week.

I took a quaking breath, trying to calm the rage threatening to consume me. "And in exchange, you betrayed your team. How did you do it? Did you plant listening devices before you defected?"

He shook his battered head emphatically. "I didn't need to. He knew everything already. Where the house was, who they were, all of it. I swear."

"But he made you prove yourself, didn't he? He put you on the ambush to see if you would do what he ordered."

At this, Jais said nothing.

I heaved a breath, feeling a surge of anger rising in my chest. "You don't have survivor's guilt, Caspian—you're a fucking traitor. Which car did you hit, the one with me, Karma, and Ian, or the one with the team?"

"The one with the team. They made me stand on the side of the road and fire before anyone else did. To make sure I wouldn't miss on purpose."

"So Boss saw *you*. That's how he gave the Midnight call before a shot was fired."

His hands clenched into fists before falling loose again. "Their fates were already sealed, David. If I didn't shoot, the only difference is that I would have been killed, too."

"Funny, because that's what's about to happen now. Fucking hilarious."

"You need to listen to me, David. We're both in very deep. You can't go back alone, or they'll—"

"I know. I could have kept my mouth shut and pretended I didn't know who you were. It's too late for me to save Boss's team, anyway. Or Karma."

He nodded in agreement. "Exactly. So we'll work together. This never happened. I'll make sure you get promoted in the Outfit, and in return you save my life right now."

"I don't need your life, Caspian. I need your meeting."

His expression fell, and a warm breeze coasted over the hilltop as he stared at me. "You don't think you can actually get to him."

"I can, and I will."

"He's had more assassination attempts than Hitler."

"Not by me."

"Listen, David. If you get close to him, it's because he wants you to. He doesn't let things happen by accident."

"I made it this far."

"Well that's—" He stopped abruptly and smiled. Then he began laughing, his expression grotesque amid the swollen disfigurement of his left eye. "Of course! You're dead no matter what you do. He knows you're coming. It's the only possible explanation."

"The only explanation for what?"

He locked eyes with me. "I didn't pick you for this job, David. He did."

I felt my hands tense on the rifle. "Tell me how."

"When you were in that interview room, I wasn't asking the questions. They filmed it, and someone on the other end did the talking. And chose you. I've never heard of that happening on an interview before, but it happened with you."

"Why should I believe anything you say?"

"Why would I have picked you over all the experienced candidates? Why would anyone?" He began laughing again. "It all makes sense, doesn't it? The two of us from the same team, out here at the end of the world? We're rats in a maze, and he wanted to see what would happen. He's probably watching right now..." He began scanning the sky, then looked at me with a haunted expression, the color draining from his face.

"It doesn't matter anymore, David. We're all damned. But he must have something very special planned for you."

His right foot suddenly advanced one step toward me, and then he slowly dragged the left leg alongside it in an eerie, limping stagger, grimacing with the effort.

I said, "I'm going to kill him, Caspian. And I'm sorry you won't be around to see that."

Ophie again, speaking as he held the knife to Luka's throat.

Say hello to Caspian for us.

I shot him four times, once for each of the teammates he betrayed.

After he'd fallen, I gave him a final bullet for me.

* * *

I hurled the AK-47 off the hilltop with one arm, watching it spin out of view before the distant clattering of its impact rang up from below.

Then I stood alone, my left hand and the case it held stained with blood. My body felt exhausted, almost on the brink of physical collapse. But my mind was the sky after the storm, clearer than ever before, vivid and free of the dark shadows accumulated after the team's death.

I checked my watch and looked to the horizon's edge for an approaching helicopter, instead seeing that the huge bird of prey I'd spotted before the gunfight was now soaring high above me, surveying the hilltop. Glancing at the crater made by the mortar impact, I dwelled on what Caspian had said and wondered if I was proceeding into certain death.

One way or the other, I probably was.

If he was telling the truth, if the Handler really did know the identities of everyone on Boss's team and the location of the team house, then the Handler surely knew about me as well. It was the only way to explain my dead teammates' words reverberating in the interview room, quoted flawlessly by someone unknown as I faced myself in the mirror.

And if so, who could be responsible but Ian?

Then there was the Silver Widow. Jais had been right about everything in our mission brief, with the sole exception of describing her as elderly when the woman I'd met was not yet old enough to drink. Was she one of the Handler's agents sent to test my true intentions? Or had her most suggestive words—or mine, for that matter—existed in my own mind, the outcome of whatever substance I had smoked in her presence?

It didn't matter, I thought. I'd stay on the path until its end, secure in the knowledge that death waited whether I was successful in killing the Handler or not. Even if I somehow escaped, even if I was inexplicably granted mercy and released into the world, what then?

I recalled visiting Boss after the final dinner we shared together. I had entered his room to find him crying without shame, holding a photograph of young twin daughters, certain of his imminent death. His final wish for me was to take my share of the money, get married, and start a family. To compartmentalize everything I'd done in combat, just as, he assured me, veterans had been doing since the dawn of war.

But there was no longer any space for me in this world.

My sleep was a broken wasteland, my hearing an endless high-pitched ringing from gunshots and explosions. Forever transformed by war, my mind would never return to domestic routines. I had never hunted an animal in my life, yet I had been hunting humans since I was nineteen. I was good for nothing except combat—combat, as I had told Sergio, that I would take however I could get it. No matter where I went in life or what I did, even if Laila took me back, even if I found someone new, no matter how many children I had or how happy I could become in daylight hours—the grandest home I could ever attain would nonetheless transform into the same space where I was the only one awake, the only creature wading through the darkness, negotiating time and space back to the bottle so I could sleep at last.

The specific memories of war and loss and death were tangible, definable, coherent in form if not meaning. But the nothingness that pulled me awake in the depth of night, and would continue to do so for life, did not have the definition to be resisted. It was the formless vapor that evaded my best attempts to avoid it. No matter what I did, it would seep back in, reclaiming my mind and soul in the endless fog of darkness.

It didn't matter how much longer I survived this journey—whether a day or a decade or ten, the length changed nothing about my situation. The darkness had claimed me long ago, and any other details about the extent of my life or lack thereof were meaningless by contrast.

Just as Boss had vowed to me, I would meet my end with open eyes.

It hurt to kill the man I knew as Jais, despite the truth of his betrayal. This sin added to the tally, to Boss's team and Karma, to the pain that kept building like a pyramid of human skulls that I continued to stack. I let the pain wash over me in that moment, as I always had. I drenched myself in it, immersed myself in it, wrung it out of my heart like a dishtowel soaked in blood because I had nothing else to give.

In my mind, I wanted to kill the Handler.

At my core, I wanted to kill myself.

Onward I would trudge, continuing my march toward the Handler's distant figure, enduring the sleepless nights of true isolation that would continue to occur at intervals unknown. My own life was the endless sandy road dividing the pines ahead in perfect symmetry all the way to the night's horizon.

Until it didn't.

* * *

I heard a chopper's rotor blades approaching. Turning east, I caught my first glimpse of a helicopter in the distance.

I set my Galil on the ground and walked to the center of the hilltop, extending my right arm straight out at my side in a prearranged signal for the recovery team.

The helicopter swerved away and then banked toward me, circling my position a hundred feet overhead. I saw it was a gleaming white Eurocopter with two men seated shoulder to shoulder inside the open door, their rifle barrels sweeping the area below. The aircraft vanished behind me while I stood motionless.

Turning, I watched the helicopter sweep back into view on my opposite side. This time its engine scaled back from full throttle as it began a sharp descent toward me.

The pilot transitioned to a near-hover a few meters over the boulder-strewn hilltop, inching downward to expertly place a single skid on a patch of open ground. The rotor wash whipped sand and debris until the aircraft had settled into its hover, at which point both shooters climbed out.

They wore ball caps and sunglasses, their faces covered by *shemaghs* as they approached me with M4 assault rifles at the ready. One man stepped sideways to maintain his aim on me as the other lowered his rifle on the sling, placing one gloved palm firmly on my sternum and the other on my upper back as he swept downward to search for a suicide vest. Then he frisked my arms and legs before raising an arm to give the all-clear to the crew on board the aircraft. Finally, he grasped my shoulder and arm and led me toward the open door of the helicopter.

I walked to the skid and set the case atop the metal floor, the handcuff links stretching taut as I climbed on board the vibrating aircraft. A medic immediately directed me to sit on the floor facing the pilots.

"Are you hurt?" he yelled over the throbbing noise of the rotors.

"No," I replied, but the medic nonetheless began sliding his hands across my body, this time checking for injuries—broken bones, bleeding, or anything else that could have escaped the notice of a patient in shock.

I let the medic do his job and watched the two shooters shuffle toward the aircraft, carrying Jais's body between them. They slid the corpse atop the metal floor of the helicopter, then climbed inside and returned to their seats. One gave the pilots a thumbs up as the aircraft slowly lurched off the hilltop. Its nose dipped toward the earth amid the thundering *wop* of rotor blades gaining traction against the air, propelling us forward and upward into the sky.

The flight medic shouted something to me that I didn't acknowledge. Instead, I watched the hills slip by as we gained altitude and banked sharply northeast toward Mogadishu.

RETURN

Contra mundum

-Against the world

12

January 1, 2009
1,500 feet over the Complex

From my window in the small, twin-engine plane, I watched the landscape as we descended toward the airstrip.

Drenched in the pale mid-morning light of a winter sun, the scene appeared as a washed-out replica of the African terrain through which I had treaded scarcely twenty-four hours earlier. The fawn-colored sand was a more tepid shade than the red-deer hue of Somali dirt, and its far reach ended in steppes and plateaus rather than the rolling hills outside Saakow.

I observed the similarities with an amused sense of detachment. I was still filthy and battered, with my wrist chained to the blood-stained case that now rested on a bench beside me. In the enclosed space of the aircraft cabin, I could smell myself—the hideous body odor and dust of the African continent permeated my being as surely as the memories of the battles I'd once again emerged from, alive.

I could make out the Complex as we banked toward our final approach, the unmistakable outline of jagged dark brown fence that shielded it from every view except from above. The bone-white buildings were now visible, the most prominent among them a large, H-shaped structure that housed the interview room and eight planning bays. Bay Six had been used to chart the course of the Somalia mission, and another of the seven, or possibly the same one, had been used last summer to plan the annihilation of Boss's team as we tried to extricate ourselves from the chaos of assassinating the Five Heads.

And as I peered down at the buildings just before our descent, I knew without a doubt that I'd been caught.

While my time at the Complex had been relatively brief, I knew the aerial view of its premises well. After all, I'd observed it closely over the course of two dozen training jumps with Jais. This familiarity made the existence of a number of additional security measures all the more indicative that my journey toward the Handler had ended.

Sniper teams now maintained vigil atop the buildings, including the hangar. Their precision rifles faced outward toward half a dozen vehicles posted in a perimeter spanning a quarter mile beyond the fence. Additional trucks loaded with security men were positioned at both ends of the runway, while roving vehicles patrolled a mile away from the Complex's center point, circling as the outermost line of defense.

I had no reason to think any of these precautions were instituted in honor of the case chained to my wrist; it had just flown from the Dark Continent to North America with no more security than any other commercial flight would have garnered. Likewise, I had de-boarded the jet at San Antonio and been hastily escorted onto the current twin-engine plane without any sign of extraordinary protective measures. Now, at a remote location known only to those who had a reason to go there, the only possible explanation for a sudden army of protectors was the imminent arrival of a known traitor.

I vaguely wondered which threat had gotten me in the end. Was it the young woman posing as the Silver Widow, or was it Ian? Maybe the Handler's purview extended beyond what I'd conceived and both individuals had been under his employ all along. Jais had said the Outfit was at the bottom of a very long and mysterious food chain, and he had known far more about the larger organization than I ever would. Maybe I'd just negotiated a complex web of extraordinary physical risk to obtain the case while unknowingly acting as a pawn marked for death, my destiny preordained as part of a vast and unfathomable game that I'd lost before it began.

At least I'd been successful in killing the team's immediate betrayer before my end.

None of it would matter in a few minutes, I reminded myself. However I'd been exposed, whether by Ian or the Somali woman or some factor I wasn't considering, upon landing I would be tortured as badly as Luka in the basement. So be it. I had no secrets to protect other than Ian, provided he wasn't working against me in the first place. And despite his voiced concerns that he and the Indian would be hunted down and killed if I failed, I was certain that both men had taken enough precautions to ensure their own safety long before I ever traveled to Newark to make initial contact with the Outfit.

I would resist my interrogation nonetheless, my contempt absolute for the forces that reduced me to an animalistic level of day-to-day survival that began not in Africa but the moment I arrived to the Dominican Republic. I would resist them out of spite, even though I deserved every excruciating consequence of my failed attempt to infiltrate the Handler's organization. The sum total of any torture they could conjure would represent a well-deserved and long-evaded sentence for the deaths of Karma and the team.

My body jolted as the plane's wheels bounced hard on the runway. The engines quieted as we slowed for taxi, and I released a weary breath into the cabin as my fatigued body sagged in the seat.

I closed my eyes, inhaled deeply, and ran through a flash flood of visualization—from meeting Boss's team to murdering their betrayer six months later in a desolate place one hemisphere and ten time zones away.

I opened my eyes and watched the hangar door roll into view as the plane's engines slowed to idle. And in that moment, despite my impending torture and death, my singular thought was this:

Fuck it.

I stood and shuffled to the rear door, the strain of the case's weight once again pulling at my left arm. Opening the airstair, I lowered the steps down to the tarmac; the outside air felt aberrantly cold as it flowed inside the plane and chilled me to my core.

Taking a final breath, I defiantly emerged from the plane.

I searched the white walls of the hangar while inhaling exhaust from the plane's engines. The ceiling was crisscrossed with metal beams that supported the weight of an enormous American flag, its drooping ripples accumulating wide arcs of dust.

An unlikely assemblage of people stood in a loose semicircle inside the hangar, their ranks punctuated by a pair of pickups with open tailgates facing me.

Sergio and Cancer were most immediately recognizable, along with a handful of faces I vaguely recognized from my previous training at the Complex. This time, there was double their number of men and women I didn't know. Most looked like fighters by nature, with the startling exception of two unfit, academic-looking people standing awkwardly in civilian clothes—one a male with thin glasses and the other a female with frumpy long hair who could have fit in as a librarian anywhere in the world. Their eyes were fixed on the case rather than on me, their excited expressions standing out in sharp relief against the stony faces of the warriors around them.

A huge man rushed up the plane's stairs toward me, and it took me a moment to recognize him as Viggs. I stood still and waited for him to press a pistol into my throat. This time, I knew, he would drown me for good. He would cut this thing off my arm and put me back in the steel drum.

Instead, Viggs nodded and edged around me, moving into the aircraft cabin.

The pressure mounted in my mind as I lowered myself to a knee, dropping my free hand to the floor to grasp a single nylon handle at my feet.

We shuffled down the stairs together, my balance perilous between the case hanging from my left hand and the 210-pound body bag holding Caspian that Viggs and I carried between us.

Upon reaching the concrete floor, the man I knew as Cancer approached me to accept the handle of the body bag. No sooner had I handed it off to him than Sergio stepped in front of me, placing a hand firmly on my shoulder and guiding me toward the people standing directly under the American flag.

His voice was grim. "Time to give up the case."

I said nothing. The librarian and her counterpart rushed forward, the woman procuring a thin metal ring holding two studded steel keys.

As she inserted one into the cuff at my left wrist, my restraint popped. The man took the case from me without a word and eagerly rushed away with his compatriot. They vanished behind a row of warriors, making their way into one of the waiting pickups.

Sergio's eyes cast a contemptuous gaze upon mine, and his tone seemed to be testing me as he said, "David, I'm sorry about Jais."

I nodded as the pulse hammered in my brain. "So am I, Sergio. I need to shower before my debriefing. After that, do me a favor and have a bottle of Woodford and a glass delivered to Bay Six. You can bill me for it."

He shook his head without expression. "That's not going to happen. There has been a lot of suspicion about how you survived and Jais didn't."

I looked around the hangar, observing the patently unforgiving stares of the bystanders surrounding me.

Then I said, "There should be, because I'm not entirely sure I understand it myself."

"You need to start explaining, David. I can't help you if you're not going to tell me the truth."

I cast my gaze around the hangar once more. "Then I need to say something that stays between us."

Sergio nodded curtly, his aftershave vaguely detectable over the harsh winter notes of earthy desert mixed with the dusty concrete hangar floor. "Do it quickly, because you don't have much time."

I leaned toward him and whispered, "I think Jais knew something that he shouldn't have, and I'm not going to compromise it any further. The circumstances of my survival are something I will only speak of in person, directly to the Handler."

Sergio sniffed hard, his upper lip curling as he surveyed the far wall. "You've got time to shower and change, but that's it. Surely you noticed the army outside."

"Of course. I thought it was for the case."

"The army's not out there for the case; it's out there for his plane. He wants to receive your debrief in person."

I tried to stop the grin threatening to creep across my face. "Make that two glasses."

His severe eyes swung to mine. "This isn't something to be flippant about, David. If you speak to him like you did in the interview room—"

I gently touched his bicep with my left hand, noticing that my wrist was red and raw after the removal of the case that I had fought to the death to protect but would likely never see again.

Smiling, I said, "Relax, Sergio. He's going to love me."

DARK REDEMPTION: AMERICAN MERCENARY #3

David Rivers killed the man who betrayed his team.

Now, he's after the faceless mastermind who gave the order.

To the criminal world, this man is known only as the Handler.

And for the first time, he is within David's reach.

But in order to get close to the Handler, David must first serve him. This time, the task is new: not to kill a target, but to protect one.

As David negotiates a labyrinth of twisted loyalties in the violent slums of Rio de Janeiro, he realizes that the betrayal of his former teammates was just the beginning.

And nothing in David's murderous past can prepare him for what happens when he finally meets his greatest enemy face-to-face.

Get your copy today at
severnriverbooks.com/series/the-american-mercenary

ACKNOWLEDGMENTS

The team of people behind this work has expanded substantially since the last installment, and I can happily report that the story was much better for it.

Julie, my sister and content editor, once again performed heroically in the unenviable role as the only person to view the initial draft of each chapter. Her assistance in shaping the story ensured that, despite my most persistent ineptitudes, it would reach a level worthy of an outside audience.

I cannot overstate my gratitude to the growing cast of beta readers. These individuals volunteered a significant amount of their time to scour the pages of a very rough product and provide input that contributed immeasurably to the final story. Two read the book while serving on deployment overseas, one shortly before his wife gave birth, and one, after being taken to the emergency room, finished the book from a hospital bed to meet my deadline. Their input flowed in through emails, texts, phone calls, face-to-face conversations over bourbon, and choppy video connections from other continents. Throughout the process, they endlessly helped elevate and refine the manuscript. And so, I owe my deepest thanks to Amy, Aaron Cestaro, CW2 J.T. Cutler, 1SG James Dauteuil, Derek, Codename: Duchess, Gypsy113D, 1SG John "JB" Presley, Randy, James Sexton, Casey Sowa, Jon Suttle, and Ernie Young.

I sincerely hope they all volunteer to return for the third installment, because I will certainly need them all.

When the story finally required the keen eye and steady hand of a professional editor, I once again asked the best person I could: the peerless Cara Quinlan. True to form, she decimated the manuscript through a month-long series of revisions while patiently and responsively guiding my writing along the way. The pain of the meticulous editing process was far outweighed by the satisfaction of seeing the finished product exceeding my every hope and expectation.

Finally, I must honor the contributions of my beautiful and long-suffering wife, Amy. While the beta readers and editors tolerate my idiosyncrasies in small doses, Amy is forced to encounter them as part of a full-time vocation. Her endless encouragement of my writing, despite the immense amount of time it consumes, has been nothing short of incredible, and I can only hope that my abilities as an author can one day rise to the level of her support.

ABOUT THE AUTHOR

Jason Kasper is the USA Today bestselling author of the Spider Heist, American Mercenary, and Shadow Strike thriller series. Before his writing career he served in the US Army, beginning as a Ranger private and ending as a Green Beret captain. Jason is a West Point graduate and a veteran of the Afghanistan and Iraq wars, and was an avid ultramarathon runner, skydiver, and BASE jumper, all of which inspire his fiction.

Sign up for Jason Kasper's reader list at
severnriverbooks.com/authors/jason-kasper

jasonkasper@severnriverbooks.com

Printed in the United States
by Baker & Taylor Publisher Services